The Ring

and

The Box

A Sherlock Holmes Mystery
Of Ancient Egypt

By
G. L. Schulze

Published by GLS Press

Cover design support by Holli Chlebowski – Graphic Designer

Book design copyright @ Holli Chlebowski

Cover photo design by G. L. Schulze

Published in the United States of America

ISBN:13:978-0692088999

ISBN:10:0692088997

Fiction/ General/Action Adventure/Mystery

Other Books by G. L. Schulze

The Young Detectives' Mystery Series:

The Secret Treasure of Pirate's Cove – Book One
The Top Secret Secret of Teddy Rigetta – Book
   Two
The Hidden Secret of Towering Pines Manor –
   Book Three
The Secret of the Sacred Mountain – Book Four
The Secret at the Bottom of Emerson's Cove
   – Book Five
The Secret of the Skeleton Key – Book Six

Sherlock Holmes – Gray Manor
Sherlock Holmes – The Case of the Dirty Hand – A
short story published in The MX Book of New
Sherlock Holmes Stories – Part X: 2018 Annual

The Ring

and

The Box

A Sherlock Holmes Mystery of
Ancient Egypt

Chapter One

He sat as usual, in the chair near the fire reading the newspaper when the soft click of the door to Watson's private apartments caught his attention. "Going out, Watson?" he asked as Watson reached for his overcoat.

"Yes, today has been quite wearisome and I thought I would take a walk to my old neighborhood and call upon several of my patients. There are a few that cannot afford medical treatment and I have donated my time to them."

"Admirable, I am sure," Holmes said with a note of lassitude, for he'd been of the same mind. "I am expecting a visitor soon and rather wished you would be here."

"A visitor? You mean a client?"

"Perhaps," Holmes replied, folding the paper and tossing it to the table. "The telegram did not indicate whether he or she wished to retain my services. It merely stated they would like an interview."

"A mystery then? This may prove interesting."

"Yes, and I am sure we shall find out in seconds as I do hear the door downstairs now. Please stay."

The thought of a new case piqued Watson's interest. He replaced his overcoat and walked to the window. On the street below stood a grand carriage of black polished enamel with a gold crest on the door. The door was rather wide, its interior hidden by the drape closed over the glass against the outside. His gaze settled on the driver who sat tall and razor straight, his black suit and top hat impeccably worn. The reins rested loosely in his hand and were tethered to two of the most beautiful stallions Watson had ever seen. Their fine coats of blue black shone brilliant against their trappings. Watson turned to call Holmes over but a knock at the door brought his attention to the visitor who entered.

She was strikingly beautiful. Tendrils of lustrous black hair caressed her forehead and outlined her petite face beneath the silk bonnet she wore. Her face was clear and smooth. Dark blue eyes sparkled against a flawless skin of light bronze. The silk of her blue gown whispered softly and the long ties to her bonnet trailed behind as she swept into the room.

She was not tall, but her confident stride affected height. She stood for a moment, her gaze resting first on Watson then Holmes, the tapping of her silk parasol to the floor the only hint of trepidation. Her eyes finally settled on Holmes and she held out her hand to him. "Sherlock Holmes, I presume."

Holmes took her hand and with a click of his heels and a curt swift bow said, "I am Holmes, at your service, madam. This is my colleague and partner, Dr. John Watson."

"I am pleased to meet you both. I am Sharrey Princeton. A strange name, you may think, but I do believe my parents could not decide on what to call me and so chose letters from the names of their most favorite pharaohs and Sharrey it turned out to be. Now may we get down to business? There is much to discuss."

Holmes had dealt with many women during the course of his investigations, but this woman was different. She was beautiful and bold, straightforward and sensible. She piqued his interest and he smiled inwardly. "Yes, of course, please sit down. Watson, would you please ring Mrs. Hudson for tea?"

"Thank you, Mr. Holmes, for the story I am about to tell is a long one. Now, I understand that you are a consulting detective? Do you engage in other business other than consultation?" Sharrey Princeton sat in the chair indicated by Holmes, setting her handbag delicately on her lap.

"Exactly what type of business did you have in mind?" he asked.

"I would like to retain your services, and that of Dr. Watson as my escorts," she nodded in Watson's direction. "Money is not an object. I have been to the police but Inspector Lestrade has informed me there is nothing they can do about the situation as it lies not here but in Africa. But, please forgive me. I am running ahead of myself. Allow me to tell you the events from the beginning."

They waited for a few moments when Mrs. Hudson entered with a tray of steaming tea and quietly left. With a nod from Holmes, Watson poured and when all was settled, Sharrey Princeton began.

"It all began several months ago, Mr. Holmes. No, in actuality it began the day I was born. My father, Peter Princeton, is an archeologist, specializing in the ancient kingdoms and antiquities of the Egyptian pharaohs. Throughout the years he has done very well for himself, hence the status that I have been raised in and have become accustomed to. While on a dig twenty-five years ago at the site of Seti's tomb, he met and fell in love with my mother, Sari Nefrati. Within a year of their marriage my brother, James, was born to them while in Egypt and four years later I was born, also in Egypt. I am told my mother was a beautiful woman, although I would not know other than the photograph I have of her at their wedding. She died in childbirth, you see. My birth." Sharrey Princeton took a deep breath and continued.

"Apparently my father blamed me for I cannot think of any other reason for his doing what he did. As soon as it was feasible after her burial, he made the trip to England with me, yet just a babe, and deposited me in an elegant house in Wiltshire, raised by nannies and tutors. He has made it a habit of returning home only once every three or four years and never stayed very long. He was always quiet, kept to himself and hardly spoke of his work. It was as though he were on some secret mission and did not wish to speak of it. He would bring my brother, James, but their visits were so very short that I really never had an opportunity to get to know James. Either of them, really.

"Every so often I would receive a letter from either James or my father, mostly from James, but there was generally nothing spectacular or amiss with their news. Several weeks ago I received a letter from James who wrote that Father was on the verge of a discovery of immense importance. This discovery, once unveiled, would make him the most renowned archeologist of all time. I am not, nor have I ever been, interested in archeology, Mr. Holmes, and so could not understand or appreciate his profound excitement. But that was when things began to happen."

Holmes leaned slightly out of his chair. "Things began to happen?"

"Yes." Sharrey Princeton took a deep breath and glanced quickly from Watson to Holmes. She continued.

"Since these events have occurred, the newspapers both here and in Egypt have mumbled about the curses of the mummy and the curses of the pharaohs as being the cause of the events. But as a very pragmatic individual, I do not believe in curses, Mr. Holmes. If I can see it and touch it, then to me it is real. The stories of mummies and curses of pharaohs are no different than the myths and legends of the old Roman and Greek gods who created the world then fought insurmountable battles of war and love to maintain their creation and its domination.

"However, my belief is neither here nor there, Mr. Holmes. The events are as follows. Within one week of James's first letter, I received a second; also from James. He wrote that when he and Father were opening one of the canobic jars they had found in this new and exciting tomb of theirs, that when they broke the seal and removed the lid, a snake no larger than the size of a ruler leapt from the canobic jar and it was so fast that Father had just enough time to move out of the way. But it flew into the face of my father's servant who was standing behind him and bit him to death."

"My word!" Watson exclaimed.

"Just so," she nodded to Watson. "I know this sounds strange, but Father and James swear the jar had been sealed as though the seal were thousands of years old and how a snake, a small thing called a viper, could have survived inside the sealed jar would be impossible. Thousands of years, Mr. Holmes!"

"Yes, that is perplexing," Holmes remarked with a glance towards Watson.

"It doesn't end there. Sometime later I received a letter from my father. Father hardly ever wrote, and when I received this note I knew something terrible had happened. It seems that James had found some ancient scrolls in the same area as the aforementioned jar, and one evening sat down in their storage tent to begin deciphering them. At morning, my father found James slumped over the scrolls unconscious and barely breathing. The physician said he could not understand James's condition as everything about his physical being appeared normal, yet there he was in some sort of catatonic state. My father wrote that once James had been brought to bed and seen by the physician that he himself went back to the tent to roll the scrolls back up to put away and he could have sworn that some of the hieroglyphics actually moved on the parchment!"

"Actually moved? Astounding! Any explanations?" Watson asked.

"He offered none, Dr. Watson, but he did write that he quickly rolled them back up and sealed them in a container. He is afraid, Mr. Holmes. I can sense this in his letter and frankly so am I. First the servant, now James. And there is more," she held up her hand before Holmes could utter a word. "Since then my father sent me a servant, who by the way is just outside your door as we speak. This servant brought with him a gift. The servant is an Egyptian that my father says is deaf and dumb, but he frightens me, Mr. Holmes. He watches my every move, he follows me everywhere and he sleeps outside my bedroom door each night. The man is relentless and when I try to speak to him, he looks at me as though he does not understand. He may be deaf and dumb, Mr. Holmes, but he does understand. I can see it in his eyes."

"What is the gift your father sent?" Holmes asked. He barely glanced at the door.

"It is here. I have all the letters from James and my father as well, if you wish to see them." Sharrey reached inside her bag and took out a bundle of letters tied together along with a small wrapped box. Unwrapping the brown paper and removing the lid from the box she handed it to Sherlock Holmes.

Holmes took the box with great care and saw that it contained a ring. He knew, without question, that he would accept the case. "This ring is magnificent! It appears to be made entirely of gold, quite large. The emerald image on the top is of a woman, perhaps an Egyptian goddess. It has been delicately chipped and minute pieces of ruby have been added to the entire outside edge of the thing. See here, Watson, the eyes are blue diamonds and no matter in which light you turn it, the goddess is staring directly at you."

Watson took the offered box from Holmes to examine for himself. As soon as he held it in his palm, a tingling sensation moved from his hand up his arm and it seemed into his very soul. "The emerald ring is indeed beautiful and is most likely worth more than anyone could possibly imagine. But I do not believe the value of the thing is based upon its jewels. The value is most likely intrinsic in nature. The jewels may have been a sign of the degree of love of the giver to the receiver, but what the goddess stands for, the powers it possesses are its true value," Watson spoke. Where such an astounding observation came from, he could not imagine. He shook his head and a strange thought that they were going to find out just exactly what it meant rushed through it.

The tingling sensation was growing stronger, enveloping his entire being and Watson suddenly had the urge to throw the box with the ring down. With great restraint, he managed to hand it back to Holmes, who took it from his shaking hand.

"Why, Watson!" Holmes exclaimed. "Whatever is the matter?"

"I do not know, Holmes, old chap, but that thing has affected me most uncomfortably." He rubbed his hand to rid it of the tingling.

"It has affected you the same as I, Dr. Watson. Each time I hold the thing, my hand begins to tingle and I become aware of thoughts and sensations that are not my own. As if I am being transported into a trance or something. I do not like this gift and would like to be rid of it, but I am sure Berihun, my father's servant, would have my head!"

"So what exactly did you wish from me, Miss Princeton?" Holmes asked casting Watson a look of concern.

"I would like you and Dr. Watson to accompany me to Egypt. I wish to bring my father and my brother James home safely before any other tragedy may befall this archeological dig."

"Surely a private protection agency would have just the type of person you are looking for, Miss Princeton."

"I believe they would but for the fact that there is no one in the whole of England who can match your wits and cunning should the need arise. I do not wish to leave anything to chance, Mr. Holmes. If it is a matter of money, please do not fret on that account. All of your expenses will be paid in addition to your regular fees, as well as that of Dr. Watson, for I believe we will be grateful for his services in the long of it. And if that is not enough, Mr. Holmes…well…well…simply name your price."

"That is most generous of you, Miss Princeton. I see that my accompanying you means a great deal to you.

However, Egypt is far and it would take me from my other responsibilities. Let us say this, Miss Princeton. Allow me to keep the ring, only long enough to have my friend at the British Museum examine it. I shall discuss this with Watson and we shall give you our answer within, say, the next forty-eight hours?"

Miss Princeton nodded, rose abruptly and held out her hand. "Thank you Mr. Holmes. That is more than I can hope for at the moment. And you Dr. Watson, I hope you will decide to accompany Mr. Holmes and myself. We may be in need of your medical attention for my brother and quite possibly my father." She stretched her hand to Watson. "I will feel much relieved if you would accompany both Mr. Holmes and I. It appears that you and I share the same malady when holding the ring. There must be a connection somewhere. In two days, Mr. Holmes. I shall await your answer."

At the door she hesitated, turning to them once more. "Mr. Holmes, Dr. Watson, I no doubt entered your home with an air of arrogance and aloofness. I am afraid that was a ruse so you would not be able to determine the depth of my concern regarding this matter. For that I do apologize. However, I am leaving much relieved for I know we shall all be going to Egypt. Good day."

"What say you to that, Watson?" Holmes asked when the door closed.

"I am not quite sure I wish to make such a journey. I have my long time patients that I still see once a week. Furthermore, that ring, although beautiful enough, is a bad omen."

"I didn't realize you believed in curses and omens, Watson."

"I generally do not, Holmes. But it was the strangest thing. As soon as I had that ring in my hand, I had the most bizarre tingling sensation that began just there and coursed its way up my arm, encompassing my entire body. It was as if…as if…"

"Go on, as if what?"

"As if my thoughts were not my own!"

"It's the curse sure enough!" Holmes laughed.

"You may make light of this, Holmes, but mark my words. There is much danger here," Watson protested unabashed of his belittling by Holmes.

"There is danger, I agree, but am not so quick to say it is coming from the ring. I myself felt nothing. However, Miss Princeton stated she had those same sensations. Perhaps there is something. A logical explanation, I am sure. What are your plans for the remainder of the afternoon?"

"I will go so see those patients and let them know we shall be out of the country for an undetermined amount of time for I am sure we will be going to Egypt. I saw that much in your eyes." He went to the door and once more reached for his overcoat. Before leaving he asked, "And you, Holmes? What are your plans?"

"I am on my way to the British Museum. I am not sure what time I will return this evening, Watson, so dine without me."

"Very good," Watson replied.

Once Watson had gone, Holmes focused his attention once more on the box that Sharrey Princeton left on the table. He noted the brown paper wrapping which was insignificant as brown paper was an ordinary commodity used for shipping packages. There was no address or writing of any kind on it. The box, at first glance,

16

appeared to be an ordinary box. But when Holmes pulled out the magnifying glass, he discovered that the box was made of a very fine dark wood. Carved in the sides were tiny figures barely discernible, because they had been worn away, nearly smoothed clean to the wood from years of handling. The box inside was lined with a fine gold colored linen that held an exotic spicy odor, one which Holmes was unfamiliar with yet found to be very intriguing.

Holmes looked at the ring nestled inside. Again the small figures carved on the underside of the body of the thing, again nearly smoothed from the wearing. He placed it quickly inside the box, snapped the lid back on and reached for his overcoat and hat. The British Museum it was.

Chapter Two

It was nearly half past two and a fine sunny afternoon when Watson exited 221B Baker Street, his hat in his hand. He looked up and down the street, seeing no sign of a readily available cab, decided to walk. It was only a few streets to his nearest patient and after taking a deep breath of fresh air, Watson turned and started to walk. The questions that arose during Miss Princeton's visit returned. What had affected James so horribly that he was now an invalid in a catatonic state? How did that viper get inside that canobic jar if it had indeed been sealed thousands of years ago? How possibly could writing on a piece of paper actually move? And more important, why did that ring affect him so?

He shook his head, for attempting to find an answer to any of these puzzling questions was impossible. First and foremost, more information was needed and he sincerely hoped that Holmes would be able to answer some of them upon his return from the British Museum.

He completed his call on old Miss Crumbly who suffered interminably with an acutely painful condition of arthritis that twisted her hands and fingers into amazingly grotesque contortions, the joints of which would never recuperate. He collected his empty vials from her leaving a fresh vial of camphor oil and one of olive oil with instructions to mix one teaspoon of each twice a day and apply to the affected areas. A small vial of turmeric powder was also placed on the table. One teaspoon in warm water to be drunk three times a day would also help with the pain. Dr. Watson let himself out.

He turned left from her gate and began his route to his next patient when an overwhelming feeling that someone was behind him caused him to turn. But there was no one there. He searched up and down the streets, shading his eyes from the sun, but still saw nothing and no one untoward. He completed his visit with Thomas Abernathy, a young man who had been injured in the head several years before and acted only five of his thirty years, then once more took to the pavement to see his final patient that day. Once more the feeling of someone behind him caused him to turn, but once again, no one was there. Watson was perplexed. Was it just his imagination? Perhaps the ominous feeling from the ring left him unsettled. Perhaps he was imagining this feeling, this sense of foreboding. With a last look around, he continued on to the derelict cottage of Mattie Harbrook. Mattie met him at her door, hobbling with an old stick her grandson, Jonathon, had fashioned out of a discarded piece of old wood.

"Dr. Watson, good of you to come. Been watching and waiting for you. Seen just now when you turned to look behind you and saw that fellow following you jump back to hide behind those hedges there. It was like he didn't want you to know he was there, but I seen him, I sure did."

Watson sighed inwardly. "Thank you Mattie. Now what can I do for you today. That leg bothering you?"

"No more than usual. But it wouldn't hurt to have some of that yellow powder in that little bottle, Dr. Watson. Helps ease the pain a little."

"Sit and let me have a look, Mattie. Ummm…yes, it does appear to be slightly swollen today. I hope you stay off of it as much as you are able. Tonight, I want you to rest, put your leg up and put a cool cloth to it for several minutes. It will help ease the swelling. Do that along with the turmeric. Increase the turmeric tea to four times a day. I want you to do that every day, Mattie." Watson reached in his valise for his last bottle of the yellow powder.

"I will surely do that, Dr. Watson, and thank you. Now you be mindful of that man out there. I can stand and watch until you are out of sight," she offered.

"Thank you Mattie, but there will be no need to trouble yourself. I will be all right. Oh, by the by, Mr. Holmes and I will be out of town working a new case for several weeks. Should you have any problems with that leg, I will ask Dr. Pennyman to look in on you."

"Why that is kind, sir, I will remember."

"Good day, Mattie." Watson lingered outside on the pretext of returning something to his valise, taking the opportunity to discreetly look up and down the streets. But once again, he saw nothing. Despite the anxiety of being followed he was relieved to know that he was not imaging it because Mattie Harbrook had also seen the man. He retraced his steps to 221B Baker Street.

Chapter Three

Holmes stepped onto the pavement several minutes after Watson. He, too, glanced up and down the street. Hailing a passing cab he gave directions to the museum. The small box, once again wrapped in the brown paper, lay tucked inside his breast pocket. The clacking of the horse's hooves on the old cobblestoned street was rhythmic and soothing and Holmes leaned his head back and closed his eyes. The image of the weathered figures both on the box and the ring came to mind. He felt sure their meaning was a key to the issue at hand. He also felt that the ring was the key to it all.

He felt the sway of the cab as it turned easily onto Euston Road and from there right onto Tottenham Court Road. Here Holmes knew every bump on the street, every hole the carriage wheels would dip into and when the cabbie turned onto Russell Street, Holmes came alert.

The British Museum of Natural History was located just off of Cromwell Road. A rather new building by the median age of buildings in London, it was completed in 1852. Since that time the collections of antiquities had been carefully packed at their old location, moved and unpacked in their new location and set on display for the viewing public. There were now lectures that were held at the museum as well as black and white brochures available as a guide for those visiting the museum.

The cab came to an easy stop and Holmes alighted and paid the fare. He took a few moments to take in his surroundings for every instinct told him he was being watched. Several people passed him on their way into the museum and several more continued their stroll beyond. He appeared uninterested in them, fixing all his attention towards the grand architectural building that lay before him.

The great south entrance was a wonder of rising white stairs that coursed along its veranda with massive white columns rising upward supporting the marble pediment above. Reminiscent of the ancient Greek temple era the pediment at the top arched to a peak, completing the awesome scale and detail of colossal Greek architecture. The entire building, although originally constructed out of block and mortar, had been covered in a layer of Portland white stone.

His eyes wandered to the intersection where there he looked up at the old familiar rooms he once occupied on Montague Street before his move to Baker Street with John Watson. Despite the years, nothing there had changed. His curiosity seemingly satisfied, Holmes entered the south entrance off Russell Street and stepped into the main hallway. He went to a podium where a visitors' log was kept by a custodian who greeted visitors and asked them to sign in. There he asked for Dr. Sterling Jasper, who was the current curator. It was a few minutes before Dr. Jasper would arrive and Holmes took the opportunity to look around.

Directly ahead was the large reading room where exhibits changed constantly. These were generally showings of special exhibits from around the world and held for a limited time only. Off to his left was a long narrow room filled with the recently acquired sculptures of Egypt. Peering through the doorway, Holmes saw a large bust of Ramses II welcoming the visitor into a world of ancient enchantments.

"Mr. Sherlock Holmes!" Dr. Jasper came with great strides and took Holmes's hand with a firm grip. "It has been a long time since we have had the pleasure of your company at the museum. Too long, if I might add." Sterling Jasper gripped Holmes's hand and shook it with great enthusiasm. He was an extremely tall man, standing more than five inches over Holmes. His hair was black, parted down the center and slicked to his head on either side. A small, thin moustache lined his upper lip, accentuating the long patrician nose pronounced at the center of his face. His thin lips parted in a wide smile and his brown eyes sparkled with excitement at seeing his old friend once more.

"Yes it has, Mr. Jasper, and I do apologize. This is not a social visit. I am here on business," Holmes replied.

"I see. And does that include an interest in Ramses?" Jasper indicated the sculpted head Holmes had been viewing.

"I am not sure if it includes this Ramses, although interesting enough. I see the curator position appears to be working well for you."

"Yes it is, Holmes old friend. Come. Before we set down to your business, let us have a cup of tea. My office is this way. I could not have wished for a finer opportunity in life," Jasper spoke, leading Holmes to his office. "The museum is my life, Holmes, and I love everything about it. We are constantly acquiring new artifacts, our lectures are going well and we receive more and more visitors every day. There is talk already that perhaps we should expand the building. Come this way. Here we are and I see the water is hot, tea is ready and

…sit…sit. We have so much to catch up on." Jasper poured tea at the sideboard of his office and once served, pulled a chair next to Holmes. He heaved a sigh and said, "For now, I am through. It is your turn. Fill me in. What is this new business of yours and how may I be of assistance."

Holmes set his cup to the side and reached inside his pocket. He removed the brown wrap and handed the small box to Jasper.

Jasper drew his breath in sharply, a slight whistle issued from the gap in his front teeth. He took the box carefully from Holmes. Holding it in the palm of his hand, he turned it this way and that. "Where on earth did you get this, Holmes?" he whispered in awe.

"A client came to me. She told me she had received this from her father recently. She does not know anything about Egyptian antiquities, has no idea of its worth or history. I would like to know because I feel this item holds the key to this case."

"What you have here," Jasper looked wide-eyed to Holmes, "is an ancient Egyptian relic that even I know nothing about. Since the work of being curator consumes all my time, I have very little time to delve into these antiquities as I once did. However, you are in a bit of luck. We have a Professor Horatio Simpkins who, although a bit of an eccentric, is one of the leading authorities on Egyptian artifacts here in England. Come. We shall mount the stairs to our Egyptian galleries proper. Professor Simpkins has a workroom off of the gallery floor where he appears to reside, if you understand my meaning. He never leaves the place or so it seems. Very dedicated."

"The box is intriguing, Holmes," Jasper said as they mounted the stairs.

"Yes, do you see the figures there on the sides? Those same figures are carved on the underside of the ring inside," Holmes added.

"A ring? It is a scarab ring? They generally tend to be," Jasper queried.

"As a matter of fact, no. It contains a carving of what appears to be a woman, possibly a goddess. It is a beautiful thing. But let's meet this Professor Simpkins and learn what he has to tell us before we get too far ahead of ourselves. Is that him?" Holmes indicated a squat, heavyset man in a doorway at the far end of the room.

They had entered into a large room of marbled floors and pillars where pedestals of pottery and jewels were displayed. Here and there were the sarcophagi of linen wrapped mummies.

"Yes it is." The excitement of the box caused Jasper to forget himself and he shouted across the room, "Professor! Professor Simpkins!" Surprised even at his own audacity, he quickly put the back of his hand to his red face.

Simpkins was a short and very overweight, bald man who grew up under the tyrannical dominance of his grandmother and was now frightened of his own shadow. He wore heavy, round glasses, thick concave chunks of glass that made his eyes appear as small buttons. He was a constant bundle of nerves, his eyes twitching, his fingers tapping, and when he spoke he rambled on nonstop until someone finally did stop him. At the sound of Jasper's shout, Simpkins jumped from the table where he had been working and knocked the chair to the floor. He stumbled back, caught his balance and reached to right the chair. "I do apologize, you startled me, Mr. Jasper," he called back.

Approaching the workroom, Jasper said, "I should apologize. There are several visitors about and I should not have shouted, but my excitement is difficult to contain. I would like you to meet Sherlock Holmes, investigating detective. Holmes, this is our Professor Simpkins."

Simpkins wiped his hands along his white lab coat, not because they were dirty, but because he perspired constantly. Being in the company of anybody scared the wits out of Simpkins and he immediately became a bundle of uncontrolled nerves. He shook hands with Holmes, apologizing for his moist hands. "I have heard of you, Mr. Holmes. Your cases are legend, so pleased to meet you."

"I have heard good things of you also, Professor. I have brought you a piece of Egypt that may interest you. Jasper? The box." Holmes said mindful of the beads of sweat standing out on Simpkins's bald head.

"Come, let us step into the Professor's workroom so as not to disturb the visitors." Jasper said. There were several people viewing the great urns and one elderly woman elegantly dressed nearby viewing the recently acquired sarcophagus of an unknown mummy had looked up when Jasper shouted. She immediately recognized the man who accompanied him as Sherlock Holmes. Catching Jasper's attention, she nodded to him, he nodded back quickly and ushered Holmes into the workroom.

Closing the door Jasper said, "That woman near the sarcophagus is Mrs. Agnes Carmichael. Of the Wiltshire Carmichaels? Very wealthy, very close to the royal house.

She is a patron of the museum and an avid lover of Egyptian antiquities. I shudder to think that I may have caused her distress with my outburst and I shall offer her my personal apologies later. But now," his eyes lit up once more, "see what Holmes has brought us, Professor Simpkins."

Jasper held out his hand and unclasped his fingers. The brown wrap fell away from the box. Simpkin's breath exploded from his lungs when he caught sight of the small ebony box which lay there. He swiped the top of his head with the sleeve of his coat.

"May I...I..touch it?" he whispered, his fingers twitching over the thing.

"Yes, of course. We have brought this to you for examination and your conclusion," Jasper said. "Note the small figures on the sides, Professor Simpkins."

Simpkins's fingertips touched the box and he jerked them back. His eyes were blinking uncontrollably and his breathing was in short gasps. He almost dared not touch the box, but his excitement for it was overwhelming. His fingers stretched, grasping the box as though he were taking up a delicate piece of thinly carved crystal. Holding his breath, he carried it to his work table and set it down with loving care.

Simpkins's work table was immaculate. Rows of relics yet to be cleaned and studied lined the right end of the space. On the left were rows of tubes and vials of cleaning solutions along with small bowls and brushes and a neatly stacked pile of clean, dry cotton cloths. Directly in front of them was the magnifying lens and bright lights that Simpkins used to study the artifacts and properly catalog and code them to their respective ages of time and place. Now, under the lens, Simpkins turned the box over and held his breath. "Oh my…oh my…this is most unbelievable! Oh my…"

"What? What is it?" cried Holmes at the heavy man's elbow.

Now, in his own element, Simpkins demeanor changed. Where minutes before he was an uncontrollable bundle of nerves, now he was precise, conscise and confident. He stared at the box and said, "This box! First let's begin with the box. This is what is known as the pharaoh's treasure box. This particular box has been carved from a single block of wood. The wood is a black wood of ancient Egypt called the African Black or Iron Wood. It is a type of ebony wood found only in the savannah regions of the woodlands of tropical Africa and its importation to other regions was restricted for the house of the pharaoh only. It is a very heavy wood, difficult to carve, but it is a hard wood and once carved would last a lifetime. As, of course, is indicated by the fact that we have it in our possession!" Simpkins exclaimed.

"And the figures?" Holmes asked.

"I am afraid that even with this high a magnitude of lens, the hieroglyphics which are carved on the sides have become so worn that I cannot readily discern their meaning. Yet!" Simpkins looked to Holmes and took a deep breath. "This does not mean, that given time, I should…but this does mean…however…this item is old. Very old, I am thinking, and I cannot be sure without testing and studying and some thorough cleaning. I am thinking that this dates as far back as the fourth dynasty, possibly from the reign of King Snofru, or Snefru as he is more commonly known. I cannot be sure, but the hieroglyphics appear to be from that dynasty. There has never been anything found from that pharaoh and if this is…oh my…the last figure looks like a bird…" Simpkins removed his glasses and bent to the box, his eyes merely inches away. "Amazing! Simply amazing!"

"All right. That's the box…"

Simpkins's head flew back and he grappled for his glasses. "That's the box! How dare you say that!" He sputtered, fumbling to get his glasses on. "Do you realize the significance of this box? Its importance not only to Egypt, but to the entire archeological community? Do you realize how much history, ancient history you have been carelessly holding in your pocket, Mr. Holmes, with no regard to its importance or archeological value?" Simpkins shouted.

"No I do not, nor do I care as ancient Egyptian artifacts do not interest me. What does interest me is the history, how it relates to my case, and if you will open the box and examine the ring that is inside."

"Ring! There is a ring inside?" Once more the man's face turned a bright red. "Oh my good Lord!" he stuttered.

"Open the box!" Holmes insisted.

"Yes…yes…the box." Simpkins turned once more to the box on the table and lifted off the lid. His heart raced and the air expelled from his lungs so fast he nearly fainted. Jasper quickly pulled a chair and made him sit down.

"Are you all right, Simpkins?" he asked.

"Yes…oh yes. I am fine. This ring, the box…it is more than I could ever have hoped to see in my days at the museum. But look here…" he carefully shifted the ring to the side of the box. "The inside of the box has been lined with a very delicate linen which has been hand dyed. Oh my!" he exclaimed.

"The linen?" Holmes asked. "What has the linen to do with anything?"

"Come, come, Mr. Holmes. You, a man who prides himself on facts and nothing but the facts, must understand the significance of everything. Everything about this item, the box, the linen, the odor, everything no matter how minute is extremely important in deciphering exactly where and who this box came from, if you wish to know the *entire* history, Mr. Holmes." Simpkins's beady eyes glared at Holmes through the thickness of his glasses.

Holmes shifted his gaze to Jasper who was inwardly smiling, enjoying Holmes's uncomfortable predicament. Only a man like Simpkins could have put him there for he did not know nor did he care or understand the political, social and investigative stature of Sherlock Holmes. "I do apologize, Mr. Simpkins, please go on," Holmes replied with an acquiescent bow.

"Ancient Egyptians actually made their clothing from plants, somewhat like today but…but…more commonly the flax plant which used to grow prolifically along the banks of the Nile. The flax plants would be pulled out of the ground by men. It had to be done by men, and pulled out…not cut. We are not sure why, yet. That is just how things were done. That was very important to them, you see. Then they would be soaked for several days and the fibers of the stalks would be beaten until softened. The fibers that resulted from this would then be spun into a thread and the threads ultimately spun into their linens. The more the soaking, the harder the beating, the finer the threads, resulting in such exquisite linens they were comparable to the texture of silk.

"The linen of this box, of course, was spun and made for royalty. Notice the gold color? The ancient Egyptians were also masters of dying cloth. This gold color was achieved by using the flowers of the carthamus plant creating a tinctorious compound. This compound was then combined with an agent called alum, a crystal that is water soluble and only found in the oasis of the now Libyan deserts. Alum is a binding agent and assured that the coloring during the dye process would not wash out. Dying linens was a very expensive process and was limited to the most high of the royal classes. This is very significant as it assures that this box was the property of royal blood."

"So you believe this box belonged to a royal member of a pharaoh's family?" Holmes asked.

"Absolutely!"exclaimed Simpkins. "Notice the odor? Another indication. The box must have been sealed for some time, for the odor is as sensuous today as the day it was sprinkled into the box. Here again, we know it belonged to a member of the royal family because this odor comes from the galbanum plant. It is an oleo resin that comes from a plant similar to fennel and it is only grown in Persia, what we now know as Iran. This means that the fragrance had to have been imported from there, again reserved only for the royal family. This particular resin had many uses. When mixed with other fragrances, it extended the 'smell' life, if you will. The smell on its own was very pleasing and sensuous and it was also burned as an incense to intensify lovemaking in the pharaoh's bedchamber. It is said that the queens would use it as a skin restorative, which is why they always looked so young and beautiful. Galbanum itself possesses its own unusual and exotic scent with its woody balsa, spicy scent. A smell of extreme sensuality and eroticism. Again, only for the house of royalty!" Simpkins closed his eyes and sniffed the box.

"And the ring?" prompted Holmes.

"The ring! Ah yes, the ring. We come to the crux of the mystery, eh Holmes?" Simpkins nudged Holmes with his elbow, a shocked look on his face when he realized what he had done. "I apologize, Mr. Holmes, I did not mean anything…"

"It is nothing. Please get on with the ring, Mr. Simpkins."

Simpkins cleared his throat, pushed up his glasses and delicately, almost lovingly extracted the ring from the box with just the tips of his thumb and forefinger. "The craftsmanship, the workmanship, the laying of the jewels, and what jewels we have! Everything from diamonds to emeralds, to the gold. This speaks to me of a royal house. The gold itself is of such a pure content, I could not be sure unless I had more time to test it, but gold this exquisite and pure would have only come from one area in Africa and that would be the region of the south which was then called Upper Egypt. Back during the Fourth Dynasty the area was called Nubia, what we call today Ethiopia, and it was a place that the Egyptian pharaohs lusted after because that area was rich with this quality of gold. The emeralds also may be from Nubia, but I would have to do quite a bit of background investigating. The diamonds are exceptional! And blue diamonds at that! Extremely rare and lustrous! This would also take some investigating but if this is what I believe it to be, these diamonds would have come from the far reaches of Africa, down along the Congo region in what is now called the Sudan. Impossible to obtain unless you were descended from the gods!" Simpkins exclaimed.

"This jeweled goddess on the top is familiar, appears to be …Isis…perhaps…let me see…see here…" he pointed to the hieroglyphics on the underside of the ring. "These are slightly different than those on the box. Give me a moment. Just here," he picked up the box once more. Reaching for a clean cotton cloth, he delicately brushed the surface dirt from the figures on the box then turned on a bright light over the magnifying lens. Squinting through the thick glasses, through the magnifier, Simpkins squealed and nearly dropped the box.

"Lord! Oh my Lord! See here? Look…look close…see the figures here? I can almost make out the first one, why it looks like a hook with a curve to the top. The second is quite unreadable and the third appears like two lines, although it may be one with the edges worn off. The last symbol appears to be a bird of some sort…good Lord!" Simpkins shouted. "Do you realize what this is? What this could actually be?"

Both Holmes and Jasper stepped back when Simpkins jumped from the chair and grabbed them by the arms. "Mr. Simpkins!" Jasper shouted. "I beg your pardon!"

"Mr. Jasper, I am so sorry!" Simpkins gasped and sputtered letting let go of Jasper's waistcoat. "It's just that these appear to be the symbols of the Pharaoh Snefru…I cannot be sure because there is so much missing…but by all accounts…Mr. Holmes. If I may…if I may be allowed to keep the box and the ring for further study. I could clean the ring and perhaps bring out the figures. I could study this more closely and possibly be able to determine exactly what these symbols are!"

"I am afraid I cannot allow that, Mr. Simpkins. It is not mine to decide," Holmes said adjusting his own rumpled sleeve.

"But...the significance of this discovery possibly being from Snefru!" Simpkins shouted. "Do you realize what this would mean for the museum? His mummy, his artifacts, nothing of significance from his dynasty has ever been discovered. This would be the first. This would be a great breakthrough!"

"I understand and share your excitement and your enthusiasm," Jasper soothed the man. "However, this article is not ours. It belongs to Mr. Holmes's client. It is for that person to decide what to do with it, Professor Simpkins."

Simpkins's face fell and tears welled behind the thick lenses. "What a discovery! And I must let it go. I am sorry, Mr. Holmes. I apologize for my behavior. It is simply that such a discovery as this...well, it is out of this world...I..." he handed the ring and the box reluctantly back to Holmes. "I do apologize. However, if it would not be too much of an inconvenience, could you say a word or two to the owner. At least to allow me to study it further?"

"That I can do, Professor Simpkins, if for no other reason than for your assistance today. I am sure my client would be receptive to the idea. Now, Mr. Jasper, Professor, I am afraid the time is late and I really must be leaving. There is a telegram I must send tonight. Thank you very much for your help. I look forward to visiting the museum when there is more time to enjoy it."

Professor Simpkins sank onto his stool, his face buried in his hands as Jasper walked Holmes to the front entrance. "I apologize for Professor Simpkins. He is usually quiet and keeps to himself, but apparently this artifact has produced more excitement in one afternoon than in all his lifetime."

"No need for apologies, Mr. Jasper. Although rather annoying, he is certainly knowledgeable. Does he get out in the field much?"

"Not at all I'm afraid. He is, how shall I say, somewhat paranoid of others. He is an extreme recluse, prefers working by himself. He is one of the best if not the best in his field. With others, he is a complete nothing. He prefers his solitude with his artifacts. Works out well for the museum."

"I will keep my word and speak of this to my client. Thank you again, Mr. Jasper." Holmes descended the stairs and hailed a cab at the next street. He found a telegraph office and sent Sharrey Princeton a note simply stating, *we will be going to Egypt*. He thought back to the events of the day. That the same woman viewing the Egyptian collection was one of those that had passed him near his cab at the entrance to the museum, earlier. This surely was not a coincidence. Holmes did not believe in coincidences.

Chapter Four

Watson had retired to his room for the evening. He'd just finished the final chapter of the book he was reading when he heard the unmistakable sound of Holmes's return. The hour was late and rather than disturb him, Watson decided to wait until morning to let him know he had been followed. He put the book on the nightstand and turned the lights off, determined to get a good rest.

It was only a matter of seconds when his thoughts returned to the strange tingling sensation that had coursed up his arm earlier that day. The feeling was so real he jumped up and turned the lights back on, staring at his hands as if expecting to see the ring embedded in the palms. Shaken, he decided to leave the lights on.

Early the following morning a telegram arrived for Holmes. Watson tapped on the door to Holmes's private quarters and was puzzled when he received no answer. He felt sure he had heard Holmes return the evening before so he called out, "Telegram, Holmes, are you there? Shall I order breakfast?"

The door flew open and Holmes took the telegram from Watson. "Yes, Watson and a hearty breakfast at that, I am famished. Ah, I see Miss Princeton has answered. She states she knew we were going to Egypt and had already booked us passage on the steamer the *Sunda I,* a ship of the Peninsular & Oriental Steam Navigation Company. We depart on Saturday."

39

"The *Sunda*?" Watson queried over his shoulder. He called down to Mrs. Hudson for the breakfast, returned saying, "Why, that is an old steamer and generally used for mail delivery, if I am correct."

"You are, but I am sure Miss Princeton has her reasons. Have you taken care of your patients then, Watson?"

"Yes, thank you for asking. And since you have reminded me, it may be important for you to know that I was being followed yesterday. At first I thought I might have been imagining the feeling, for each time I turned, there was no one there. But when I reached my last patient, Mattie Harbrook, she told me herself she saw a man following me."

"I expected nothing less, Watson. I myself had the same experience and I met with the same outcome as you. It was a good chance that Mattie Harbrook saw the man. Did she perchance say what he looked like?"

"No she did not for she was overly concerned for my welfare in the matter. What are we to do about that?"

"Nothing we can do, but remain vigilant. I believe they do not know exactly what they are looking for and were only following us for information. If they were after something they would have made an attempt yesterday. The steamer trip is twelve days. We are only at the beginning of the journey. Be sure to pack well for we will be gone for several months."

"I am nearly there. When exactly are we to meet Miss Princeton and where?"

"Southampton. The *Sunda* sails out of the eastern dock, Number 121 and is noted for its timeliness. Eight a.m. sharp. We will be ready, Watson, alert and ready."

"And what of your visit to the museum, Holmes? Did you obtain any useful information regarding the items?"

"Yes, of course. Thank you, Mrs. Hudson," Holmes said as Mrs. Hudson set the tray on the table. "And by the way, Watson and I will be leaving on Saturday and will be gone for several months. Please see to it that our mail is collected and the apartments are seen to."

"Of course, Mr. Holmes, don't I always?" replied Mrs. Hudson. "Any other particular orders you wish to give while you are at it this morning?"

Holmes laughed. "No, that will be all."

"As you wish, and have a safe trip," Mrs. Hudson returned good naturedly, then left.

"Now we get to it, Watson," Holmes said reaching for the cup of tea. "The professor at the museum seems to believe this box and ring are from the Pharaoh Snefru. He states that nothing has been discovered regarding this pharaoh and anything remotely close to his dynasty would be a great archeological find. This pharaoh lived during the fourth dynasty, whatever that means. Whatever that means, it is definitely an ancient Egyptian relic and one I am sure would rouse the curiosity and desires of any antiquity collector."

"Do you suppose that is what James was referring to in his in letter to his sister about his father finding something that would make him the most prominent archeologist of all time?"

"That is quite possible," Holmes said, "but we won't know about that until we actually are able to have a talk with her father, Professor James Princeton. As much as I dislike admitting this, Inspector Lestrade was correct in telling Miss Princeton he had no jurisdiction on the case.

The problem began in Egypt and to Egypt we must go. By the way, hand me my red leather book."

Watson retrieved the book from the second shelf and Holmes quickly turned the pages to P where he read aloud, "Ah, here it is. Peter Princeton. Son of the late Lord Byron Henry James Princeton and Lady Emilie Cordington Princeton. Money there, eh Watson? Only child, educated London University, Professor of Egyptian archeology and antiquities, has spent his entire life in Egypt, widowed, has two children, James and Sharrey. Has done some work for the British Museum quite some time ago, but most of his expeditions have been sponsored and paid for by the family money." Holmes slammed the book shut. "Well, that settles that!"

"Settles what, Holmes," Watson poured himself more tea.

"That he is in need of no man's help where it concerns financial matters. It explains Miss Princeton's obvious wealth. It also explains how he has been able to finance his expeditions. Most archeologists have a difficult time persuading anyone to sponsor their digs."

"That is true. But let us return to Professor Simpkins. Was there anything regarding the markings?"

"He did say they were hieroglyphics and could make out some of the figures or writings as they are, but could not actually determine for a positive fact what they meant or who they belonged to. He needed more time to study them and truth be told, Watson, I wish we had that time for I believe Professor Simpkins would most likely be the one to break the code on these ancient writings."

"Did he mention anything about the strange sensations both Miss Princeton and I experienced when we held the ring?"

"No, sorry old chap, I am afraid that subject was never discussed."

"Never discussed? Did you not think that would be an integral part of the puzzle, Holmes?" Watson cried.

"Why yes, it probably is, but I am sure those symptoms you and Miss Princeton have experienced can be explained away by science and reason once we have arrived in Egypt. Just as we will be able to explain what affected James and sent him into a catatonic state. Do not forget, Watson, there was nothing to indicate the parchment he was studying had anything to do with his condition. He was seated in a tent. A structure anyone or anything had access to at any time."

"That is quite true," Watson conceded. "But what about the father who said the writing actually moved?"

"We only have an exhausted and distraught father's word on the thing. He obviously was overly tired from working at the dig all day, compounded by anxiety over the perplexing condition of his son. Easily explained," Holmes shrugged.

"But the ring?" Watson exclaimed. "You yourself saw the effect! And why did it not affect you? Have you an explanation for that? No! Of course not! It did not involve you directly therefore you have not given that aspect a second thought, have you?"

"Why, Watson! Why are you so disturbed about this?"

"I really do not know, Holmes. Perhaps because it affected me and not you. Perhaps because the feeling was so strange that it was as if it belonged to someone else and not to me. Perhaps because I believe that it had something to do with the outcome of this case and you callously dismiss it as though Miss Princeton and I are some old wives having a fit of the vapors!"

Holmes broke into a bout of laughter that only heightened Watson's anger.

"Laugh! Go ahead and laugh, Holmes! Mark my words, it all has something to do with the ring!"

"I am sure it does, old chap. Obviously Peter Princeton has had these trinkets for quite some time and I am sure are of a personal nature, else he would have boasted his find and the ring and the box would already be in a private collection or in a museum. But some event has occurred in Egypt that has caused Peter Princeton to panic, which is why he sent them to his daughter in the first place. Not only did he send the items, he sent them with a bodyguard. There is more to this than just the ring or the box and you are correct in that this case is all to do with that ring and the box."

"But…but…" sputtered Watson.

"But calm yourself. You yourself have admitted in not believing in curses. Your strange sensation regarding the ring can be explained away, just as James's condition. You will recall in one of my cases, I believe you called it, the dying detective, where a poisonous residue was placed on the tip of a hinge and when that hinge was touched in order to open the box, it jabbed the flesh, depositing the poison, thereby killing the person opening it. It's all about logistics and science, Watson. However, one cannot guess or make assumptions. We must remain calm and reason this out rationally and logically."

Watson leaned back in his chair and conceded. "You may be correct, Holmes. I do apologize for my behavior. It is simply that whatever the ring does to cause that sensation I would not like to see what happens to whoever wears the thing. It almost changes one's mind about curses."

"We don't know if it is a curse or even what the curse is now, do we Watson? So how can it be a curse? Logical. Rational. Watson, we will find the answer."

"I do hope you are right, Holmes, before someone really gets hurt."

Chapter Five

The cool morning mist rising off the water was already dissipating and the sun's rays were moving rapidly across the bay. The Southampton docks were bustling and noisy. Passengers arriving early were milling about, chatting to friends and relatives before boarding. Seamen were busy inspecting the ship both inside and out one final time before the *Sunda I* was to sail. Dock workers were busy loading the cargo onto platforms that were then hoisted into the air and swung over the opening of the cargo compartments of the ship. From there they were lowered and the stevedores took over. There were areas for fruits and vegetables, areas for storage of meats and areas for crates of personal items being shipped overseas. Most important was the mail cargo hold. A wide compartment now filled with boxes and crates of mail and objects for shipment to the African and Asian continents as contracted by the British government.

Holmes and Watson stopped to survey the bustle. Watson spoke, "You know, it has been some time since I have sailed. The last time I was on a ship was when I was returning home and out of my head with fever after being wounded in the war."

"Things have changed much in many respects and in others they remain the same. Take for instance this dock. Why I remember when Southampton was a minor shipping port. Since the establishment of the Royal Pier, this port city has grown by leaps and bounds. Ships from all over the world dock here moving not only goods and mail but also people. Travel has become much too easy for this generation, Watson, and once you see the comfort that has been established on these ships, one wonders why anyone would want to stay aground."

Holmes wove his way through the crowd, Watson followed. He said, "I understand that the P & O is one of the first shipping lines to have steam generated electricity installed on their ships."

"Yes, it appears that nothing is too good for their passengers. Ah, here we are, the gangway. We shall board and hope that Miss Princeton makes the departure time."

Jostling through the throng of people moving up and down on the gangway, Holmes and Watson struggled with their bags. A young boy pushed through the crowds and rushed upon them. "Your bags, sirs? I am a porter for the ship."

"Thank you," Holmes said. The boy secured their bags and hustled through the crowd calling out. "S'cuse me, make way, gentlemen boarding. S'cuse me."

The crowd gradually parted, eyeing the young boy pushing through, his arms heavy with travel bags and soon Watson and Holmes stood on the deck The purser was there verifying passengers arriving against the ship's manifest and directing them to their quarters.

"Sherlock Holmes and Dr. John Watson," Holmes said when the purser raised his eyes without lifting his head. The eyes quickly bent again. The pen scrolled down the pages, stopped and made a mark. "Yes, here you are sir, Sherlock Holmes, A Deck, berth 152," the purser said without a glance up, flipping more pages. "And here you are, Dr. John Watson, A Deck, berth 154. Here's your keys welcome aboard gentlemen. Next!" he shouted.

"One moment, can you tell me if you have a Sharrey Princeton?" Holmes asked.

"Sharrey Princeton, let me look. Yes, A Deck berth 153 right across the hall, sir. She's already arrived and on board, sir. Next!"

"There is no need to be concerned she will make the departure, Holmes. She is eager to be on the way. Come, we have several flights to ascend. The bags are getting heavy for our young man there."

"No need to worry about me, sir. I can handle this. If you like, I am available for you during your voyage. All you need do is request the service of Whittingham. That's me, sir, Whittingham. Whatever you need, just ask for me. I'll get it for you," the boy beamed. Appearing to be about fifteen, Whittingham was a tall boy with dimpled cheeks and a scruff of curly brown hair. The thin reedy arms and legs belayed the strength of the youth, for he hefted the bags without much effort. "Which way, sir?"

"Whittingham," Holmes eyed the lad up and down and replied, "A Deck." The boy grinned and shuffled on ahead of them.

They had not gone far when a deep voice boomed behind them. "Sherlock Holmes!" Holmes and Watson turned. "Captain Harkin Thadpole, sirs, at your service. When I saw your names on my passenger manifest, I knew I must meet you." Captain Thadpole gripped Holmes's hand and shook it vigorously. "And this is Dr. Watson, I presume? Wonderful to meet you, wonderful to meet you both. Come, I shall escort you to your berths. I am very pleased to have such renowned citizens aboard my ship. You will take note that we have made many updates, added many new passenger berths, which are now known as suites, and they have been refurbished quite handsomely."

"That is kind of you, Captain," Watson said.

"Oh, not at all, Dr. Watson, it is my pleasure. I have been captain of the *Sunda I* for many years and it pleases me to have you aboard. Ah, here we are. A Deck, very new, very posh. Your rooms are just here. And what is this boy hanging about?"

"Whittingham, sir. I have been spoken for by these two gentlemen, sir," the boy quickly answered.

"Is that so?" Thadpole cast a shrewd look to Holmes and Watson.

"If that is correct with ship's policy, yes," Watson answered.

"Yes, of course, of course. I hope you have a most enjoyable voyage, sirs. And if you would be so kind as to join me for dinner at the captain's table. We serve at seven sharp. Good day to you both." Thadpole tipped his captain's hat and strode back towards the stairs.

"Well, that certainly was nice of him..." Watson began when a door behind him opened quickly.

"Mr. Holmes and Dr. Watson!" Sharrey Princeton exclaimed. "I see you have made it aboard and that you have met the captain. A truly jolly fellow, and a very apt seaman from what I am told."

"Miss Princeton, good to see you have made it here safely," Holmes remarked. "I thought you were berthed in 153?"

"Safely? Whyever should I not?"

"I only meant that with the bustle on the docks, the passengers and the cargo, very tumultuous."

"Shar?" a voice called from within the room.

"Oh, Mr. Holmes, this is my dear friend Minerva Rothman. I have asked her to accompany me. I did not care for the idea of traveling alone. Minnie, this is Sherlock Holmes and Dr. Watson. And yes, I am in 153. It is, however, being inspected by my father's servant. He is making sure it is safe. Can you believe it, Mr. Holmes?"

Holmes eyed the burly man that exited the door of 153. He was very tall, his head and face clean shaven. When he emerged into the hall, the strong powerful frame beneath the white robes he wore was evident. He bowed to Miss Princeton and cast a suspicious look over Holmes and Watson. Apparently satisfied, he stepped aside from the door, crossed his arms about his chest and stood vigilant.

"I see no harm in that, Miss Princeton. And where will he be staying?"

"Outside my door, of course. I have booked him a room but he refuses to leave. He will most likely stand outside my room day and night for the entire voyage and cause me great distress."

"Again, I see no harm in that, Miss Princeton as long as it does not interfere with the other passengers on this deck," Holmes said. "If you would excuse us," Holmes made an apologetic nod. "We have only just arrived and would like to become settled. Shall we join for lunch once the ship has gotten under way?"

"That will be fine and now that our rooms are safe, Minnie and I will do the same. Come, Minnie," Sharrey Princeton giggled. She closed the door, leaving Berihun standing in the hall.

Watson began sorting through his luggage, laying things on the bed to put away. He stretched and looked about. The room was not too small, holding a bed in its center with a nightstand and a lamp near that. In the corner was a reading chair with newspapers already placed on the seat. Above that was a small porthole that allowed a filtered light into the room and at the next corner was a wardrobe. He opened the doors and saw that it was spacious and held shelves at the sides for his small personal toiletries. On the opposite wall of the bed were two doors. The first he opened, peered inside and saw that it was a very small washroom. He was surprised when the second door opened onto another door. Opening that, he saw Sherlock Holmes standing there.

"I see we have adjoining suites, Watson. Saves time should we need to discuss events," Holmes remarked without looking over.

"Yes, it will I daresay. The rooms are small but adequate and we apparently have our own personal bathroom. Miss Princeton must have paid well for these accommodations."

"She did say money was no object. Apparently that is so," Holmes finished looking about the room.

"Look, I hope you don't mind, Holmes, but it is nearly time to set sail. I am going up on deck and partake of the departure festivities. I shall finish my unpacking later."

"Suit yourself, I have thinking to do." Holmes shut the door.

Watson, experienced in the eccentricities of Sherlock Holmes, simply shrugged and reached for his overcoat and hat. With a furtive up and down look at the big man standing guard in the hall, he strode quickly past Berihun and exited the stairs to the starboard deck. Billows of black smoke rose from the smokestacks and the thunderous blurting of the ships horn signaled that the ship had already departed the dock, its soft swaying movement told Watson they were leaving the harbor.

Watson reached the deck still crowded with travelers waving and shouting to those on shore. Pulling his hat tight to his head, he shouldered his way through until he was near the prow. The stretch of water that lay before him was breathtaking. He leaned over the railing, watching the ship clear the harbor, her great mass slipping through the water effortlessly. Waves rippled from her bow, ebbing towards the shore weakening until they became a gentle slap against its banks. The shoreline slipped away, those that remained on the docks were soon a tiny speck. Slowly, one by one the passengers left the deck, departing to their rooms to unpack and rest. The voyage would be a long one.

Watson stayed. The laughter and shouting of the passengers dwindled until gone and all that remained was that of the ship gaining momentum coursing effortlessly through the water with the occasional screech of the gulls following them seaward. The cool mist sprayed off the prow and wet his face. Watson closed his eyes and took in a deep breath of the scent of open water. He had been in a high pitch fever when returning from the war and had not been able to enjoy that voyage when he returned home. Now, he stood a man alone against the wind, a wind that would soon turn cold when they exited the Channel and steered their course through the Atlantic. He shuddered. The sort of shudder one feels is an omen of bad things to come.

When he finally turned to retrace his steps, he found the deck empty of all passengers, but standing near the door to A Deck was Whittingham, a quick smile spread across his face when he caught Watson's attention.

Whittingham hurried forward. "Is there something wrong, sir?"

"No…no," Watson replied. "I was simply enjoying our departure. I will be returning to my room, young man. Must unpack you know."

"No need, sir. Done for you," Whittingham grinned. He pulled the door open and bowed to Watson.

"Thank you, Whittingham. Now before we go much further, you will tell me the truth. Are you a porter on this ship?"

Whittingham grew afraid. He wet his lips and thought about running, but despite his fear of the outcome, he held his ground. "No, sir. I am on board with my mother and four brothers. We are lodged below with the other poor passengers, sir. We barely had enough money for our fare. We are going to the canal where my father has been working. I am sorry, sir. I did not mean to deceive you."

"You did not. I gathered by Captain Thadpole's response to your presence that something was amiss. No matter. You shall serve as our porter, Whittingham. You have done well thus far."

"Thank you, sir. I will do you proud. Anything, anything, sir, I shall be ready. I will sleep in the stairwell out of sight. I will hear when you are up and will knock on your door if you need anything."

"No need to sleep in the stairwell, boy. Simply stop by several times during the course of the day and if we are in need of anything, we shall leave a card on the door. Will that do?"

"Yes, sir, thank you, sir."

"Here you are then. We will not be requiring your services for the remainder of the day." Watson handed the boy a shilling. Overly much and extravagant, was the thought that passed through his mind, but then, Miss Princeton was paying all costs. Furthermore, this was to be his first true holiday. No case to solve, no villains to apprehend. Simply accompany a young lady and her friend to Africa. What could be more simpler than that?

"A shilling! Thank you, sir!" The boy ran down the stairs out of sight but stopped on the next landing. He looked at the shilling in his hand. He thought about the lie he had just told to Dr. Watson. There was no mother. There were no brothers. There was no father that worked at the canal. Whittingham was alone and he was a stowaway. He stared at the shilling and feared that he would be found out. He had nowhere to go. Whittingham retraced his steps to the A Deck landing. Peering through the glass on the door, he counted the doors until he was sure he memorized which ones were for Dr. Watson and Sherlock Holmes. Of course, he chided himself. It was much easier than that. They were the ones opposite from the big man in the hall. He sat himself down in the corner, leaned his head to the wall and closed his eyes.

Chapter Six

The doors between the rooms were open and Holmes shouted out to Watson who went in to find the man bent over the small black box. "You have not returned it to Miss Princeton?"

"Not yet, Watson, look here. I have been studying these two objects and they are unrelated."

"Unrelated? What do you mean?"

"The box, according to Professor Simpkins, may be from the reign of Egypt's Pharaoh Snefru. Now, according to this book I purchased, Snefru reigned about 2575 B.C. and what I am able to gather by these pictures is that his iconic symbol was a staff, a spoon shape, an eye shape and a bird. According to this book it translates to Snefru is Shining. Examine it carefully under the magnifying lens, come here, under the bright light," Holmes called to Watson, handing him the lens. "Look closely there. They are eroded but you can just make out the staff, an up and down shape, then two parallel lines somewhat curved and an image of a bird. Professor Simpkins was on to something with that."

"Yes, I see what you mean," Watson mused.

"But when you look at the symbols on the ring, they are different." Holmes held out the ring.

Watson took a step backwards and stared at the ring for several long seconds. "If you don't mind," he finally managed, "I would rather not touch the ring."

"Watson!" Holmes exclaimed. "It's just a ring!"

"To you perhaps, to me it is a symbol of evil," Watson countered. "But, to prove a point, give me the thing."

Holmes handed Watson the ring, a triumphant look on his face. Taking it in hand, Watson bent to the light with the magnifying lens. "I see what you mean, Holmes. It is difficult to make out the markings but they do appear to be different. Perhaps once we rendezvous in Egypt with Miss Princeton's father he will be able to shed some light on this matter. Strange though. I am not experiencing any discomfort with the ring this time." Watson shifted the weight of the ring from one hand to the other. He grasped it into his fist then uncurled his fingers. There was no recurrence of the strange tingling at all.

"It may have been a moment of excitement that brought about a dizzy spell the first time. Or," Holmes eyed the small black box sitting on the table, "it was not the ring at all."

"But at the apartment, you yourself observed my reaction when I held the thing in my hand!" Watson exclaimed.

"What I observed in our living quarters was you taking up the box with the ring inside and holding onto it. It is a matter of simple deduction, old chap. If the ring does not affect you now as on that day, then a simple test would support the theory that it may be the box. It is worth the experiment."

"Everything to you is an experiment! I personally wish not to relive the moment. I was most discomforted by it and very unnerved."

"An experiment, Watson, else we will never know. You took up the ring willingly enough. Why not take up the box."

Watson scowled at him, conceding that Holmes may be correct, which of course he always was. He took a deep breath and nervously reached for the box. He placed the thing in the palm of his hand and bent to study it but almost immediately the tingle began to travel up his arm, throughout his entire body. The light dimmed and his vision blurred and it was impossible to move, to throw down the box, to loose it from his grasp. A murmuring of voices filled the mist, vague and indistinct in the far distance; a chanting of a promise whispered that Watson could not understand. He fought the creeping darkness but to no avail. The magnifying lens fell from his grasp to the table as the very air grew thick and he could not breathe. Watson swayed.

"Watson!" Holmes cried. He grasped the box from Watson's palm and tossed it to the table just as Watson's knees buckled. He assisted him to the bed then quickly drew a glass of water. "Here, quick man, take a drink," Holmes tipped the glass to Watson's lips. It was several minutes before the dizziness settled and Watson dared open his eyes.

"Are you all right, old man?" Holmes asked, shaken by what had just happened.

"Yes, I apologize for that. I don't know what came over me, but I can say beyond a shadow of a doubt it was that box."

"It is I who should apologize, old friend. It seems there is something to this sensation that overtakes you when you touch that box. And at best, now we know it is the box. There must be a logical explanation…a reaction to the wood or something which may warrant further study…or do you suppose there really is a curse?"

"Ah, I see you are making light again, Holmes," Watson sat up unsteadily. He swung his feet over the side of the bed and swayed, immediately steadied by the sure grasp of his friend's hand at his shoulder. He gripped his head in his hands for it was throbbing mercilessly. "But I shall keep away from it nonetheless. Forgive me if I do not join you and Miss Princeton for lunch or tea. I have a terrible headache and will just lie down this afternoon. Perhaps you could have the dining room send a tray?"

"Of course. I will extend your apologies. Allow me to help you. You are still a bit disoriented."

"Thank you, Holmes, I do feel so. A quiet lie down will do me good. I will talk with you later."

With a concerned last look at his friend, Holmes returned to his own room. He went to the table where the box lay tipped on its side, the tiny figures carved there obscured by time yet had endured. He stared at it for quite some time before picking it up. What could the logical explanation be that would account for the strange way it affected Watson? Holmes was more determined than ever to find out. Watson was, after all, his closest friend and by all appearances, the box was the enemy. He shook his head once more at the thing before replacing the ring in the ebony box and the box in his pocket.

Stepping across the hall, he tapped the door to Miss Princeton's room. Berihun, still standing there, said not a word. "Are you ready, Miss Princeton?"

"Yes, of course," she looked around. "Dr. Watson is not joining us?"

"He begs forgiveness, but is suffering from an acute headache. He is lying down but should be able to join us for dinner tonight. Shall we?"

"Let me get my shawl, and Minnie. I am sure she would like to join us."

The dining room was a very large area and was already more than half filled with passengers chatting and laughing. Holmes's keen eyes quickly noted everything and everyone in the room but did not readily see anything untoward. At his request, the waiter seated them at a small table on the deck which offered a little more privacy and a lot less noise. Holmes took the seat facing the dining hall. He requested a tray be sent to Watson's room then turned his attention to the ladies. "There, that is done. Now, Miss Princeton, is there anything else you wish to tell me about your father and your brother? Anything at all?"

"Not much more to tell, Mr. Holmes," Sharrey replied. "I do not know much about them other than when they would visit. I do remember James was a quiet boy who kept mostly to himself. I believe he was, is, much like Father. So involved and engrossed with his work he hardly sees the world around him. Although, the last time he was home, he did appear to notice Minnie!"

"Sharrey! You do tease!" Minnie Rothman blushed.

"Did he, Miss Rothman?" Holmes asked.

"I'm sure it wasn't really me he noticed, as Sharrey has said. I…well…it's just that I was really interested in some of the relics he brought home and that seemed to spur him on. He spoke mostly of his excavations and his finds. He hardly noticed I was there at all except for being the audience. Some of his work is quite interesting."

"So you take an interest in archeology where Miss Princeton does not?"

"I find it interesting, but I would not go so far as to wish to become an archeologist, Mr. Holmes. I find it difficult to keep up with the events of the present day let alone be concerned with what happened thousands of years ago."

"In that, I could not agree with you more," Holmes smiled. "Ah, here we are. Let us enjoy this wonderful lunch, then if you would excuse me I have much to do."

"Excuse me sir, but there is…well…a man…standing just there," the waiter set the plates on the table and indicted towards the hall, "and he appears to be interested in this table."

"No need to fret, he is my bodyguard. If you would kindly see he gets the tray we inquired about earlier, we will try to ignore that he is there," Sharrey Princeton grimaced.

"As you wish, miss," the waiter replied.

Lunch continued with the casual talk about the ship and the voyage and once the table had been cleared and a fresh pot of tea brought, Holmes found an opportunity to excuse himself. With Berihun standing guard, he returned to his room. He looked in on Watson who was sound asleep on the bed, the untouched tray still on the side table. Closing the door, he turned on the bedside lamp and reached for the box in his pocket. He took it in hand and studied it very carefully. There were no hidden latches or catches that could possibly hold a drop of opiate, causing the strange reactions in Watson. He picked up the ring and again inspected it for catches or latches or tiny pieces of metal protruding that may hold the key to the strange malady that appeared to affect Miss Princeton. The metal was genuine gold and the jewels were true. There was nothing to indicate a physical or logical explanation why the ring and the box should affect these two people as they did.

He was relieved he had convinced Miss Princeton into letting him keep the ring for the duration of the voyage; not only for safekeeping, but also to study. But what further was there to study? The thing was a test of the fine craftsmanship of the Egyptian artisan. And over the years, the small figures engraved on the underside had nearly been obliterated, until they appeared as no more than dimples. He put the ring back into the box, clapped the lid on and tucked it into his breast pocket once more. There was much more to this ring and its box and Sherlock Holmes was more than ever determined to find out. He uttered a mild curse at the length of the voyage, for much could happen in the next eleven days: both to Sharrey Princeton and to her father.

Chapter Seven

Several days passed before Watson felt nearly himself. He kept to his room, taking his meals in and reading. The thought of the box and the effect it had on him frightened him. How could an inanimate object wield a power no one could understand or explain? And up to this point, Holmes had offered none either. Truly disappointed, Watson was beginning to fear that Holmes had lost his touch, for surely any other case would have been solved already. But was this truly a case? Their purpose was to accompany Miss Princeton back to Egypt and convince her father and brother to return to England before any further injury could be sustained. Was the riddle of the box and the ring becoming a case unto its own? Of course, Holmes would make it so. And no, he did not believe in curses. At least up this point, he did not.

By the fourth day, feeling restless from his self-imposed quarantine, Watson decided to stroll about the ship. He found himself near the bridge and saw the captain at the helm. He popped his head in the doorway. "Captain Thadpole. May I have your permission to enter?"

"Ah yes, Dr. Watson! Come in my good man, come in. I was taken to understand that the voyage was not treating you very well. Seasick, perhaps."

"Not at all, Captain, I assure you. I have traveled several times abroad and have never been seasick. It may have been something I picked up back in London and it simply caught up with me. I am well now, thank you."

"Very good, I am happy to hear of it. How are your friends enjoying the voyage?"

"It appears to be going well. The ladies are anxious to arrive in Egypt of course, for Miss Princeton's father is an archeologist there, as well as her brother. Miss Rothman is her very dear friend and traveling companion and appears to be enjoying it very much, also."

"And your stowaway?"

"Stowaway!" Watson exclaimed. "Why whoever are you speaking of?"

"The boy, of course, the young lad who carried your bags. He is not a registered passenger, Dr. Watson. I have only allowed him to roam the ship as a courtesy to you and Mr. Holmes, as you had spoken for him."

"I apologize, Captain, we did not know. He told us he was traveling with his mother to the canal where his father was working."

"An orphan, no doubt, a runaway from the workhouse or orphanage," Thadpole said. "I cannot blame him for that. However, stowaways are not allowed and I am afraid he will have to be dealt with by the law when we reach the Straits."

"But Captain Thadpole, surely there is something we can do about it. He is not a problem is he?"

"Not at all, Dr. Watson. He has made himself most helpful to the passengers. He knows his way about being a servant and is extremely polite and has a quick wit about him. He does very well. I have had many compliments from the passengers regarding his courtesy and helpfulness."

"Then might we come to some sort of an arrangement. Let us say this. Is there anywhere open, a berth, a small storage room, any place where he can be put up? I will be more than happy to pay his fare."

"And why would you bother yourself with such a lad, Dr. Watson? A runaway from the workhouse; an orphan, a liar and a stowaway? Surely these belittle his character."

"That may be so, Captain, but you must admit those circumstances alone would lend itself to lying and running way. There are too many such young people that have been abandoned, sent to orphanages, or made to work in the workhouses. It is a most tragic state of affairs, Captain. The poverty and depravation and sometimes cruelty of these places is not conducive to producing an upstanding member of society. No, Captain, I have seen firsthand what such places do to these children. It is not good."

"As this is a special request for you and Mr. Holmes, I shall have my purser find your lad quarters and perhaps some cleaning chores in the kitchen. We will hire him on as a temporary worker and his passage will be paid through such. After all, the passengers already believe him to be an employee of the ship and if truth be told, I rather like the lad myself."

"Thank you, Captain, I am in your debt. When we reach our destination I will take Whittingham in hand and make a determination regarding his welfare. Now, I believe I will step back to the deck and find myself a place to enjoy the sun and a good book. I have been shut away in my room for far too long. Good day, Captain."

Watson strolled casually about,a book tucked beneath his elbow, a blanket wrapped over his arm. There were few people out, for the wind had a bite to it but Watson did not mind. He had been sequestered in his room for four days recovering from the effects of the box, until he could stand the stuffiness and the four walls closing in about him no longer.

He glanced up to see the red, white and blue of the British flag whipping about in the wind when a man in a brown tweed coat, the collar pulled high about his face to ward off the wind, bumped him. "Excuse me, sir," a muffled voice uttered and the brown tweed faded into the shadows.

"Not a problem," Watson began, but the man disappeared almost immediately. Shrugging, Watson found a deserted chair on the deck and made himself comfortable beneath a large sun umbrella, thinking no more of the incident. The book he was reading soon fell and rose steadily against his chest where he lay it down. He let out a sigh of contentment and surveyed all that lay before him.

The sky was a deep blue with long tendrils of translucent clouds swiftly blowing across its expanse. They accumulated here and there into masses of billowing dusky gray in the distance, a sure sign of an oncoming storm. Near the horizon where the ocean met the sky, a narrow band of deep gunmetal gray deepened and stretched as though the wind were tugging it against its will. White caps were forming on the water, the waves rising and falling like the beat of a heart.

"Dr. Watson!" Sharrey Princeton called out. She strode quickly towards Watson and sat down beside him, wrapping her shawl tightly about her. Berihun, who had been behind her, remained near the rail, out of hearing but very much within sight. "I do hope you are feeling much better."

"I am, Miss Princeton, thank you for your concern, and it is good of you to join me," Watson said. "I was reading but decided to simply enjoy the scenery. The green of this ocean is an amazing color, nearly like the color of those emeralds on your ring, I daresay."

"Now that you mention it, it does appear to be so," she replied. "And I am happy that you have brought up the ring, Dr. Watson, for it has been on my mind also."

"In what way?"

"I hope you do not think less of Mr. Holmes, but we were discussing the ring the other day and he told me of your reaction to the box when you picked it up to examine it. I wanted to tell you that the same thing happens to me every time I hold the ring. When I first received it from my father, I was fascinated by its beauty and frankly surprised that he would send me such a fine item. After all, it is an Egyptian artifact, probably found in one of those wretched tombs he crawls into, but to send such an item to me? I began to wonder about it. And when I picked up the ring to try it on, I had the strangest sensations. Tingling of a strange nature seemed to course up my arm and throughout my entire being, Dr. Watson. My head swooned and the lights seemed to shudder and it was as if I could not breathe. Thank goodness Minnie was with me for she immediately came to my aid and tore the ring from my grasp. It was what appeared to save me, Dr. Watson."

"That is very strange. I mean, how the ring affects you is the same exact manner in which the box affects me."

"But the strangest thing happened later when I was resting. Minnie took the ring and actually put it on her finger. I was afraid for I feared the same reaction, but it did not affect her at all. She greatly admired the ring and made a silly comment, under her breath really, something like, 'I can't wait until you are mine, or when you are mine' or…oh I cannot remember her exact words. But I thought strange at the time. I know you look at me as though I were losing my mind."

"Of course not, Miss Princeton for as I have said, those same strange sensations are happening to me. It was as though… if I kept hold onto the box, that my being was no longer mine, but belonged to someone else. There! It is out. Now it is you who look at me as though I have lost my mind. I have not told this to Mr. Holmes, for he would surely believe this to be so."

"Your secret is safe with me, for that is exactly my thought, Dr. Watson. I believe, for both of our sakes, we should stay away from that ring and the box as far as is possible."

"I agree." Watson nodded and turned his gaze back to the ocean. "I have never been on such a voyage to the far reaches of the earth. Oh, do not misunderstand me for I have traveled with Mr. Holmes several times back and forth to the continent, and have fought in the Great War in Afghanistan. But one was on the business of a friend and colleague and the other for the service and honor of our country. There was no time for frivolous lounging or scenery, albeit we are going to Egypt for your brother and father. Yet, it is as though I am experiencing my first holiday! This…" Watson swept his arm to include the vastness around him, "this is truly magnificent!"

Sharrey Princeton smiled and rose. "Well then Dr. Watson, I shall leave you to enjoy your view. Sitting out here with the impending storm coming is a bit too chilly for me. I simply wished to speak to you of the ring and that I have done. I look forward to your company at dinner tonight? Good. Until later."

"Good day, Miss Princeton," Watson said. He watched her stroll away until she was out of sight, grateful to see Berihun not far behind. He peered into the shadows for he thought he saw something, or someone there, watching Miss Princeton. Or perhaps... watching him? But after a moment he saw there was nothing there at all, just shadows. He turned his attention back to the ocean. The wind was rising, blowing cooler, the ocean a bit rougher. White caps of foam frothed atop the waves rolling across the empty vastness of water, disappearing into the surf only to reappear on the next wave. Watson smiled and leaned back, closing his eyes. The afternoon waned and the yellowing sun slowly inched its way toward the west amidst the rich colors of maroon and orange, getting lost in the encroaching gray. He pulled up the blanket across his knees and dozed. And the day slipped past.

"I see you are enjoying the voyage, Watson!" Holmes exclaimed when Watson entered his room one afternoon.

"Yes I am, Holmes. I was happy to see our mail stops at Lisbon and Cadiz were brief. I am eager to be on land once more and discover what Egypt has to offer. There are only three more days before we reach Gibraltar. I am looking forward to that. I have been doing some research on that. The books I purchased before leaving London have proven to be very interesting reading. Perhaps..." but Watson's sentence was cut short by a piercing scream.

Both men jumped for the door at once. Holmes flung it open and they bolted out. They stopped abruptly, nearly colliding with Berihun standing as still as a statue blocking the entry of Sharrey Princeton's door. Holmes grabbed the back of Berihun's robes, steadying him, preventing him from sprawling headlong into the path of danger. Whittingham was running down the hall towards them. Inside, Sharrey Princeton was pressed against the wall.

Only a moment earlier, Sharrey Princeton had grimaced at Berihun behind her before she entered her room. She closed the door with a loud thump, tossing her shawl to the bed. Disturbed by her entrance, the action brought a large cobra slithering from beneath the bed. Its body rose, towering in the air, its head swelled, its body swaying. The long serpents tongue flicked in and out of its mouth and the oval translucent eyes flared angrily. Sharrey screamed and threw herself against the wall, putting her fist to her mouth to stifle her screams.

Berihun had thrown open the door with such force it hit the wall behind and bounced back, saving his life, for the cobra lunged at the moving object, striking the door instead of the servant. Berihun's eyes widened in horror. Watson reached out seizing Whittingham by the arm, drawing him back out of the way. The room grew deathly still. No one moved, no one dared even breathe and the cobra swayed to and fro in a mesmerizing motion, facing Sharrey Princeton once more.

"What is it, Dr. Watson?" Whittingham cried. He struggled to free his arm, managing to peer around the door jamb. "Oh!" he gasped.

"Be very quiet, boy. Any sudden noise or movement will incite that snake to strike," Watson whispered. "Step back slowly, way back, out of the way. We may have to move quickly."

Berihun's eyes never left the menacing threat of the cobra. He'd been in similar situations time and time again in his country and he knew very well what to do.

He very slowly raised a hand to his lips and whispered to Sharrey Princeton, "Be still! Do not move, my Queen." He raised his other arm to his chest just as slowly. The movement caught the snake's attention and the thing slithered about to face him. Berihun eased himself into the room positioning himself between Sharrey and the snake. The cobra reared higher, standing as tall as a man, and lunged at Berihun. With lightning speed, the big man sprang forward, dodging to his left. He reached out, catching the snake around the back of its head with one hand and with the other grabbed the slithering body that now coiled itself, twisting and writhing around his hand and arm. Sharrey screamed and cowered back into the wall.

"Quick!" Holmes shouted. "Watson! Stay with the girl. Berihun! With me!"

Whittingham pressed himself flat to the wall, eyes wide with terror at the site of Holmes and Berihun racing from the room, the large snake twisting furiously to free itself. Once past, the boy sped into the room, shouting. "It's all right, miss! It's gone!"

"Step aside, Whittingham," Watson said, reaching for the woman. "Help me get her to the bed. Then be quick boy, fetch some water then run into my room and fetch my doctor's valise. It is in the wardrobe, on the bottom to the left."

"I am all right, Dr. Watson. Frightened! Terribly frightened that is all," Sharrey said pushing herself up.

Whittingham returned with the valise with Minnie Rothman close behind him.

"Sharrey! What happened? I saw Mr. Holmes and that man with something awful…"

"It was a big snake, miss!" Whittingham burst out. "It almost bit and killed Miss Princeton but that big man saved her life. Did you see that, Dr. Watson? Did you see how fast he was? He was faster than the snake, catching it like that! And strong!"

"Yes, yes, Whittingham, we saw the entire episode and I am sure we do not need you reminding Miss Princeton of the danger she was in!"

"I meant no disrespect, miss."

"Oh, I will never forget the danger I was in and thanks to Berihun, thanks to all of you, I am sitting here alive. Shaking, but alive. I thank you all very much. There is one thing I have learned from this."

"Keep your door locked?" Whittingham queried.

"No," she managed a weak smile, "that I will never underestimate the value of Berihun as a bodyguard again. Thank you, Dr. Watson. I will not need a sedative. Your being here is sufficient and now that Minnie is back, I shall be all right."

Chapter Eight

Holmes moved swiftly to open the doors, standing far out of the way, while Berihun followed, the snake writhing and twisting, the large head struggling in the tight grip of the big man. They rushed across the empty deck to the rail.

"Here, man!" Holmes shouted. "I'll grab the body and twist it from your arm. Once we are freed of that, we shall, on the count of three, toss the thing into the ocean. Ready?" Holmes shouted.

"It is your wish. I am ready," Berihun answered. With a thrust on the third count, Holmes let go of the writhing body and Berihun flung the snake high into the air, its body twisting and curling in a futile attempt to grasp onto something. It rose in the air, spiraling as it came down before landing in the ocean with an inaudible splash. Gripping the rail, both Holmes and Berihun held their breath and watched the snake sink out of sight.

"So you can speak," Holmes said finally turning to the man.

"When there is a need, sir," the man answered, bowing his head. "Now, there is no further need." Berihun bowed once more to Holmes, turned and returned to his post outside Sharrey Princeton's door.

"She is shaken but unharmed, Holmes," Watson said when Holmes returned. "I have offered her a sedative but she refuses to take it. She insists she is much stronger than the simpering frail woman we men believe her to be.

Furthermore, her friend Miss Rothman is now with her. How do you suppose that snake got there? After all, we all have our own keys. And where would such a thing come from aboard a ship in the middle of the ocean in the first place?"

"Either she forgot to lock the door when she left earlier or someone else opened it. I stopped to inspect the door, but was unable to determine if it had been broken into or broken in two when Berihun burst it open. I must admit at this point, Watson, that someone is out to harm Miss Princeton for the snake on board is no accident. Anyone could have brought it aboard because luggage is not inspected. It also could have been brought on board through the loading docks. One thing is for certain; whoever it was that brought it aboard and put it in Miss Princeton's room tells us the situation has escalated and that her life is in danger. It is no longer a matter of escorting her to Egypt, Watson."

"It has become an official case, then Holmes?"

"Indeed."

"They are after the ring and the box?"

"Yes they are, and I fear their attempts at attaining their goal will continue. It now confirms why you and I were being followed the day Miss Princeton left us the thing. Whoever is up to this did not know which of us had it and so followed us both."

"It also makes sense, Holmes, that whoever followed us then is on board now."

"Yes, we must remain vigilant, Watson. Apparently our villain has discovered pertinent information regarding the ring and the box and now feels the items must be taken no matter the cost."

"Are the ring and the box that important? Could that information be why Peter Princeton sent the items to his daughter in the first place?"

"Yes on both counts, and it must be information of crucial importance for these attacks to escalate."

"But to actually harm Miss Princeton? Who do you suppose it might be?"

"I need not remind you that Miss Rothman also has a key and their rooms connect as ours do. And, there is the porter."

"But Miss Rothman is her friend, Holmes. You do not suspect her of foul play, do you? And the porter has been employed on this ship for years, what motive would he have?"

"We must suspect someone, or rather perhaps everyone. Neither you nor I nor Berihun have any reason or motive to harm her. As attested to by Berihun's selfless act of ridding us of the snake. We can definitely rule him out as a suspect. If not Miss Rothman, then who? And the porter, I daresay, for a price, would sell his mother's soul."

"I do not suspect her. There must be someone else on the ship that we are unaware of. It may well be one of the boarding passengers that came on during our routine mail stops at the ports. We did take on some additional passengers, you know."

"That is so," Holmes replied. "And a possible explanation. But we shall not restrict the possibilities to just these few. I have been watching, but have not seen anyone taking any particular interest in Miss Princeton."

"That is strange that you mention that. Why just the other day when I was reading on the deck, I thought I saw someone in the shadows but dismissed it as fancy. And that same day, there was a man who actually bumped into me there. I could not see his face for he had his collar up, but I thought it odd at the time as there were not many passengers out and there was plenty of room to walk about."

"He said nothing?"

"Only mumbled an apology."

"Were you missing anything?"

"Excuse me?"

"Generally a bump of that sort is not random, Watson. It is quite the handy means by which pickpockets employ their trade."

"I don't believe anything was missing, but then I was not carrying anything but my book and a blanket."

"It could have been one of those that are following us. Keeping to the shadows, watching us. This one was brave enough to try to pick your pockets to determine if you were in possession of the ring and the box."

"Yes, but why me?"

"Most likely because you were alone and it was the perfect opportunity. Generally Miss Rothman and Miss Princeton are together with Berihun not too far behind, or are in our company. Furthermore, it would be too dangerous to accost a woman with so many others around. A man accidentally bumping into a man is not out of the ordinary. This one had to be sure you did not have the items. Either way, they, whoever they are, are becoming increasingly bolder the closer we get to Egypt."

"I should say not just bolder, but dangerous."

"Indeed. Are you sure it was a man that bumped you?"

"I cannot say. As I said, his collar was up, the hat pulled low. The voice was muffled in the folds of the collar and, if truth be told, I really paid no never mind to it."

"You'll have to pay closer attention to every detail every day. Following us was the first step. They have come to the conclusion that one of the three of us has possession of the thing. First bumping into you. That satisfied their curiosity that you did not have it. Now this attempt on Miss Princeton's life. I am sure whoever it was first searched her room and found nothing there. Placing the snake was their next step to rid themselves of Sharrey Princeton and narrow the prospects of who has the ring and the box. They most likely left the snake after searching her quarters and not finding the items."

"They certainly had ample time to do so."

"That is true. Another point of interest, is that Miss Rothman is never very far away from Miss Princeton, yet today, she was nowhere to be seen. Where was she by the way?"

"After you left, Miss Rothman entered the room just as I was administering to Miss Princeton. Apparently she and Miss Princeton had been taking tea. Miss Princeton decided to return to her room and Miss Rothman remained to finish her tea. She was returning to the room when she saw you and Berihun rushing towards the railing with something in your grasp. She returned immediately and was in an obvious state of distress knowing that her friend could have been killed by that snake."

"Did she appear genuinely surprised and upset?"

"Yes...I believe she did...but then I was more concerned with Miss Princeton's condition than with Miss Rothman's reaction to the situation."

"Yes of course. But we know now that Berihun is not as deaf and dumb as he has made out to be. He has an excellent command of the English language, but I could not get another word out of the man."

"We must be grateful that he was there to protect Miss Princeton. By the way, did I hear him correctly? My queen? What do you suppose that was all about?"

"I don't know, but it is very curious and there is much more to this story than we have been told. And it all involves Miss Princeton and that ring."

"Yes, the ring. You know, Holmes, she came to me several days ago and described to me the very identical symptoms each time she touches the ring. Why would her father send her such an object if it is going to affect her health?"

"I don't know, but I do not believe her father feels it is a danger to her, at least not in that regard. I believe he sent it to her for safekeeping. Why else would he also include a servant to guard over her? A man who is much more than a servant. And why, since she has received this ring, has she been followed, as well as ourselves? And now the situation has become dire. Someone has actually threatened her life. The situation is escalating."

"Yes and I recall, she also mentioned that Miss Rothman was with her when she received the ring and tore the ring from her grasp when she was experiencing the strange sensations. But, the ring did not affect Miss Rothman at all. As a matter of fact, Miss Rothman put the ring on her finger and greatly admired it saying something very strange."

"Which was?"

"She said something to the effect of, when you are mine, or something of that nature. What do you suppose that is all about?"

"I do not know, but we must keep our wits about us when dealing with Miss Rothman. As with Berihun, there is more to this friend of Miss Princeton's than meets the eye."

"Such a sweet girl, Miss Rothman. It is difficult to believe there is malice in her heart."

"Times are changing, Watson, for there is malice in everyone's heart these days."

"Where are you going now?" Watson asked when Holmes started for the door.

"To see the captain. I am going to inquire about those passengers who came aboard during the mail stops at Lisbon and Cadiz."

"Very good, and I will check on Miss Princeton, although I daresay after today, Berihun will probably never close his eyes or allow anyone near her."

It was several hours before Holmes returned to the room. The look on his face told Watson there was news and not good news at that. Watson was sitting near the portal, reading one of his newly acquired books about Gibraltar when Holmes entered.

"Watson, come here. There is much to tell you." He threw off his overcoat and began to pace.

"I take it the news is not good, Holmes?" Watson queried entering Holmes's room.

"Not in the least. There is more going on aboard this small ship than the whole of London, I declare!"

"Well, out with it man!"

"I found him on the bridge in heated discussion with another man. This man, a Mr. Allistair Bridgewater, as it turns out, is co-owner of the shipping line of P & O and was just informing the captain that this would be the last voyage of the *Sunda I*. He stated it has been sold to the Sultan of Zanzibar and this is to be it. Captain Thadpole was extremely upset for this was the first news he'd received about the sale. It will be final once the *Sunda I* has reached Gibraltar. Apparently that is why Miss Princeton and the others were able to arrange our travel on board at such short notice. Gibraltar is as far as we go on this ship. That alone will pose a problem for us. Here on board, we are able to maintain our watch for the means and opportunity are limited."

"Does this mean we must make our own arrangements to go overland to Alexandria?"

"Yes, I'm afraid it does. I do not like this, Watson, I do not like this at all."

"I would suppose Captain Thadpole is angry also because now he is out of a ship."

"Mr. Bridgewater has assured him his service with the company is valued and he need not fear retirement. Thadpole appeared appeased at that news. It was the surprise of the sale that upset him most, I think."

"What else have you learned. What about other boarding passengers?"

"There were several, but as we are a mail carrier, not many. Besides, the company knew they were selling the ship at Gibraltar and therefore took on no more passengers than were going there. There were three who boarded in Lisbon, a man, a woman, and a child, a family. There was one in Cadiz, a woman traveling alone, a school teacher headed for Cairo. That was all. However, later I spoke to the purser and he told me that Miss Princeton sent a telegram to her father to let him know we were coming. He also said that her companion, Miss Rothman, sent a telegram to someone by the name of Chibale telling him the same."

"Chibale? Who would Miss Rothman know in Egypt by the name of Chibale?"

"Who would she know in Egypt at all, Watson. That is what we must learn. We will not mention this to anyone but we will keep our eyes open and be on the alert. Miss Rothman is not the sweet, innocent, young woman you thought her to be."

"Perhaps not, Holmes. But it still does not make any sense why she would try to kill her friend with such a ghastly method such as that cobra."

"No proof, no fingerprints, no evidence, Watson. The snake makes the perfect weapon. The one question remains, was it Miss Rothman and why? And if not her, than who?"

"Technically, Holmes," Watson smiled, "that's more than two questions."

"Yes, yes of course. Actually there are many more questions, but now we will deal with those two. Right now, Miss Rothman is our prime suspect but we will not rule out any others."

"Do you believe Miss Rothman capable of conspiring and scheming all on her own?"

"No I do not. If she is involved, she is involved with another party. Perhaps this Chibale character she wired. But for now, our main concern is the situation at Gibraltar. If we must travel by land to our destination, we must truly be on guard. Berihun must be brought into this."

"Do you think he will cooperate with us or even agree to work with us on this?"

"I do not see how he can refuse. After all, we are all after the same result; to keep Miss Princeton safe and alive. Here now, I will call him in and you stand watch at her door. We do not wish to leave her safety to chance."

While Holmes impressed upon Berihun the urgency to speak with him, Watson took a position outside Miss Princeton's door. Reluctantly Berihun left his post with a wary look back. But once the door was closed, Holmes began.

"See here, Berihun," he said, "Watson and I have learned some very disturbing news. The ship is to be sold once we cross the Straits and our voyage will have to be completed by caravan. I am afraid Miss Princeton's life will be in grave danger, and it will be up to you, me and Watson to see to it that she reaches her father unharmed. Watson and I are counting on your willingness to cooperate with us on this matter."

Berihun considered Holmes's proposal for some minutes before answering. "Miss Princeton's life has always been in danger since receiving the gift. I have been sent to protect her and the gift. You must understand, Mr. Holmes, there is more to Miss Princeton than you or Dr. Watson are aware. I am unable to disclose any information without the permission of the professor, her father. But, as you say, it is up to us to protect her for her life is most valuable and precious. I will do whatever is necessary, and I will not, in any way compromise my sworn oath to protect her regardless who stands in my way. Even should it turn out to be you."

Holmes blinked back his surprise. Of all the things he presumed Berihun would say, a complete paragraph in perfect English was not one of them. He checked his surprise with a clearing of the throat and said, "That is all we ask, no more, no less. It is good we are agreed on this. We will keep each other informed of events, yes?"

"Yes," Berihun answered with a slight bow. "It is my wish to know the location of the ring and the box."

"I have it here. I convinced Miss Princeton to allow me to keep it for safekeeping and for further study. It appears that was a bit of luck for I fear the ring is what the culprits are after."

"They are after the ring *and* the box, for both hold the same power. They must be one with the other and not separated for one without the other is meaningless. They must be protected as well as we protect Miss Princeton, for she is the key. I can say no more than that."

"I understand for I gathered as much. I will keep the box here for now. You, Miss Princeton, Watson and I are the only ones who know its location."

Berihun bowed to Holmes. "If that is all, I will return. Thank you, Mr. Holmes and your friend. Miss Princeton will be kept safe."

The dining room was quiet when they entered later that evening. The tables were filled, the nervous whispers circling the room about the sale of the ship had everyone on edge. Minutes passed before the captain entered. He took his place at the head table and tapped his spoon against his glass for the passengers' attention.

"Thank you all for coming. I am sure you have all heard the news of the sale of the ship and are much distressed," he began. "But I have just come from speaking with the sultan who has purchased the ship. He has graciously agreed that we continue our journey across the Straits to its destination at Alexandria and he will assume ownership there. Therefore, ladies and gentlemen, there is nothing to worry about. The *Sunda I* will continue until we have safely docked in Alexandria."

A sigh of relief echoed about the room amidst the applause. "And now, we toast to the Sultan of Zanzibar!" Captain Thadpole shouted.

"To the Sultan!" shouts rose as glasses were raised.

"That is a bit of luck don't you agree, Mr. Holmes?" Minnie Rothman asked. "I was upset fearing we might have had to travel overland to complete our journey. I hear it is a most deplorable and dirty journey."

"Yes, Miss Rothman, it is good news," Holmes said to her. "We finish the next two days of our journey in relative luxury."

"I am glad for that. The thought of going overland by caravan...ugh!" Sharrey shivered. "I understand they pack your belongings onto the backs of camels and then actually expect you to ride the beasts yourself!"

"I would wager it is much faster than walking the distance, Miss Princeton," Holmes remarked wryly.

"I suppose you are correct, Mr. Holmes," Sharrey shrugged.

"Let us have a toast of our own," Watson said. "To a safe journey and profitable end."

Chapter Nine

The *Sunda I* neared the western port at Alexandria just after dawn on the second day of leaving the Straits. The passengers were eager to be back on land. They crowded the decks shouting and laughing, their trunks and suitcases scattered about, slowing everyone. Captain Thadpole guided the ship through to the second zone where the passengers could disembark, as well as the bulk cargo could be discharged. The docks were teaming with men, women and children. Most of them dressed in the traditional white garb of the Egyptian people. They bustled to and fro helping to unload carts and camels, setting up stalls for selling their wares and worked with a constant chanting that buzzed through the hot dusty air.

Whittingham gripped the bags of Holmes and Watson and once again hustled through the crowd shouting, "Gentlemen coming through, ladies coming through, step aside please, coming through, step aside please."

"I rather enjoy having that young lad helping us, don't you Holmes?" Watson asked.

"He has been helpful, but I see no further need of him now that we have arrived," Holmes cast Watson a sly look.

"But I..."

Holmes laughed. "I know he was a stowaway, Watson. I have spoken with the captain regarding your arrangement. I find that admirable but now that we are in Egypt, what are we to do about him?"

"We could keep him on, Holmes, for pity's sake. The boy is homeless and we could always use some type of help. He's strong and willing, eager to learn and most helpful in all respects. He doesn't require much…"

"Enough said. We shall keep him on. I am not completely heartless, you know, although it puzzles me why you have taken such an interest in the homeless stowaway lad."

"Truth be told, I'm not sure. Perhaps it's because he reminds me of someone else I know; someone eager to learn all there is to learn about all there is."

Holmes could only smile at the inferred similarity between Whittingham and himself. "Once we return to London, we shall find suitable accommodations for the boy."

"Thank you Holmes. I will see to his arrangements once we are settled."

"Father! Father!" Sharrey Princeton suddenly cried out. "Excuse me, I must get by. My father is there, waiting for me!" She pushed between them threading her way through the jostling crowd and ran down the gangway.

"Father! Oh Father, it is wonderful to see you!" she cried throwing her arms about his neck.

Peter Princeton had arrived early that morning, impatiently pacing while waiting for the *Sunda I* to arrive. He was tall and lean, his face and hands tanned with that weathered leather look from spending his entire life beneath the blazing sun of the desert. His khaki trousers and shirt were stained and wrinkled from countless days of wear and the crumpled hat that usually shaded his blue eyes from the sun was now twisting anxiously between his hands.

Days earlier he'd received Sharrey's telegram informing him that she was on her way to Egypt. Alarm soon gave way to anger. James was in a catatonic state impeding the progress of the dig. With Sharrey in Egypt, the dig was not only impeded but all of their lives were in danger. Especially that of Sharrey. To compound the situation, he had to leave James and travel to Alexandria to try to turn Sharrey back, get her out of Egypt, out of danger. Why? Why had she come?

He paced the dock, his anger returning as the ship moored and the passengers began to disembark. He heard her shout and there she was running towards him. Her beauty struck him when the loosed black tresses of her hair flew back into the wind and his heart ached once more for his beloved wife, Sari Nefrati. It was a stark reminder of why he'd sent Sharrey away in the first place. His last words to Sari before she died in his arms were a promise to keep Sharrey safe. Fool! Fool that he was! His foolishness in sending those last letters to her had caused her to come to Egypt and run headlong into the path of the danger he had sent her away to avoid. And there she was. A beautiful young woman with the face of her mother, Sari, excited and lovely, running towards him with open arms.

He stood stiff and unyielding when Sharrey's arms entwined about his neck. He felt the soft brush of her lips against his cheek and peered down at her happy smiling face. His heart ached, and as much as he longed to hold her and tell her he was so pleased to see her, he knew he must not. He would not, could not, encourage her to remain in Egypt. He slowly removed her arms and stepped back. "It is good to see that you are safe, Sharrey, but why have you come? Do you not understand how unsafe it is for you here?"

"But Father, I have come to bring you and James back home. Your letters…"

"Those letters should never have been sent! I was a fool to allow that. Now you are here and the danger is at our doorstep! You should not have come!" He shouted at her, his fingers tight on her shoulders.

"Mr. Princeton, allow me to make introductions. I am Sherlock Holmes, my colleague Dr. Watson and this is Minerva…"

"Sherlock Holmes! You have brought Sherlock Holmes to Egypt! You are a foolish girl. You should have stayed home where you were safe! And you!" He turned on Berihun, his fist thrust in the big man's face. "Why did I send you to protect her in the first place if you could not even prevent her running directly into the path of danger!"

"I beg your pardon, Professor Princeton," Dr. Watson cried, "but there really is no need for the shouting. Your daughter only wished to be sure you were home and safe."

"Home and safe! I am home! I was safe! Your arrival here, *her* arrival here, has put us all in more danger than you can ever imagine!"

Sharrey drew back, mortified at her father's outburst. Tears welled in her eyes, words choked in her throat. "Had I known you disliked my presence so much, I would not have come, Father!" She took Minnie's outstretched hand and together they ran down the dock. Berihun shook his head, a piteous look upon his otherwise unreadable face and turned to follow her. "I will see she is safe."

"I will come with you," Watson said. "I cannot stand here for another minute listening to this outrage of senseless blame."

"Ah, Professor, what brings you to Alexandria?" a voice from behind called out.

Peter Princeton was taken by surprise. With the confrontation with his daughter fresh on his mind, he turned absentmindedly to the young man that approached. He was tall and of a rugged stature with skin bronzed by the sun. The eyes were nearly black, his hair, dark as the night, draped over his collar when he removed his hat. He gripped Princeton's hand and shook it vigorously. "It has been a long time since we have seen each other. Is it business that brings you here, sir?" The young man looked eagerly from one face to another. He'd been close enough to hear the confrontation between Princeton and his daughter and he made every effort to soften the tense situation.

"No, no, I have come to fetch my daughter. She has only just arrived on the *Sunda I*. She has been graciously accompanied by Sherlock Holmes here and his colleague Dr. Watson who has gone to retrieve Sharrey."

"It is a long time since I have seen Sharrey. She must be a beautiful young woman now. She was just a baby when last we met. Pleased to meet you, Mr. Holmes," the man extended a handshake to Holmes. "Yes, even here in Egypt your name is legend. I am Colter Mitanni. I am an old friend of Professor Princeton and an out of work archeologist at the moment. May I escort you to your hotel?"

"We will not be staying. I have only arrived to take Sharrey back to my dig site immediately. I have no time to make arrangements to send her home so to the dig site she must come. I must hurry back. My son, James, you know. He remains bedridden."

"I was very sorry to hear of his misfortune. If you will allow me, Professor, I'd like to accompany you and your daughter back to the site. I have no pressing matters to hold me here in Alexandria."

"That is kind of you, Colter, thank you but my site is at Dashur. Now let us assemble the luggage and be on the move. If you don't mind, Mr. Holmes, we do not need your assistance any further. My daughter is here and you have delivered her safe. I thank you."

"On the contrary, Professor Princeton. You yourself have just called attention to the acute danger she is in due to her arrival here. I am not one to leave a client before I am confident that I have done all that I can. My services are in the employ of Miss Princeton, not you. It is her decision, sir, her decision alone whether I stay or not."

Princeton turned on Holmes, his anger rising once more. The confrontation with his daughter had left him angry with himself and the sudden appearance of Colter Mitanni caught him off guard. Not wishing to cause another scene, he acquiesced and sputtered, "I stand corrected, I apologize. Let us find that girl and get on with this. I have been away from James far too long."

Whittingham, who had been standing well behind watching over the luggage, called out, "Sir, what are we to do with all of this? I can but carry half," he indicated the numerous bags and trunks that had been unloaded.

Holmes said, "Stay with the bags, Whittingham. We shall be back momentarily with porters to load them for our destination. By the way, has Dr. Watson spoken to you?"

"About what, sir?" Whittingham paled and took an anxious step back. He knew sooner or later he would be found out and would be cast out or worse yet, handed over to the local authorities. And there they were, at the end of their destination and no longer required his help. He looked about at the bustle of the port, the strange people running to and fro and wondered, where would he run to?

"About staying on with us. We may be in need of your services for a few weeks longer. Would that suit your family?"

"I am sure it would, sir, and thank you, sir," Whittingham beamed.

"Good lad." Holmes looked up to find the two ladies some distance away deep in conversation, Watson and Berihun remaining nearby. Professor Princeton and Colter Mitanni were standing near a group of workers and were now arguing a price for their time. At length they had come to an agreement for five of the men approached Holmes. "We take bags. Professor man, he pay us take to riverboat. We see to safety."

"It is all right, Holmes. They are going to carry the bags to the *Queen's Traveler*, a riverboat that sails up and down the Nile with cargo and passengers. I have booked several cabins but did not count on such a large retinue. We may be short a cabin or two. Where on earth is Sharrey?"

"I am here, Father," Sharrey, Minnie and Watson approached the group with Berihun not far behind.

"Then let's get on with it. We have a long way to travel and I must get back immediately. I have been away from James far too long. He is still in a coma state,

Sharrey, and I am at my wits end. Nothing the doctors have done has been any help."

"I am so very sorry, Father. I was not aware of your despair. Perhaps once James sees me he will improve? Or if not me, than perhaps Minnie?"

His voice softened and he immediately repented his anger, his outburst of stinging words. "If your lovely face does the trick, it will have been worth your coming. Please forgive me, my daughter. It is not you I should be angry with but myself. I should have never sent those letters. They were written in haste and have no doubt caused you undue worry. It is long time since I have had to deal with matters other than my archeology and sometimes it is much easier to blame those who are wholly innocent of circumstances and events rather than oneself. It is your safety I am most concerned with."

"I do understand, Father. I had not considered your concern for my safety for I felt I was in no danger. I was traveling with Sherlock Holmes after all. And I underestimated your concern for James, not knowing the full extent of his condition. Shall we make a new start?" Sharrey smiled and put her arm through her father's.

"It might be prudent if you would explain to us just what sort of danger she is in?" Watson said.

"Not now, for it is a rather long, hot journey and we must get to the *Queen's Traveler* before she sets sail. We will speak about this on the way. Here, there are too many ears. It is good you brought a houseboy to help with the luggage, Sharrey. Grab those smaller bags boy, and follow us," Princeton called to Whittingham. "We must hurry."

Whittingham secured the smaller bags beneath his arms and with one in each hand, followed the group who were followed by the five Egyptian men wrestling with the remainder of the bags and trunks.

They zigzagged through the cramped narrow streets, pushed through the throngs of bustling people, tugging themselves away from persistent sellers eager to ply their goods, listening to the haggling of buyers and sellers who crowded every avenue. Whittingham held tight to the bags for tiny hands tugged and grabbed at them, attempting to dislodge his grip. The air was a vibration of people singing, shouting, arguing, and laughing. The temperature soared quickly as the beating sun swelled to scorching levels.

They pushed through the crowds, past huge warehouses and granaries that rose skyward against the horizon where ships from Syria, Greece, Rome and many other foreign places could bring their agricultural products to be stored. From there, the business of buying and selling to the local merchants of Alexandria continued day and night, for the haggling over price never stopped.

Centuries before, the city of Alexandria was built by the Roman General Alexander just a short distance from the mouth of the Nile. Here, a narrow tongue of land stretched to the sea, its waters deep enough for ships to anchor with a small nearby island offering some protection from the elements. All along the Nile, merchant ships were coming and going, with some already lying at anchor in the roadstead, where they could ride the water easily enough. The roadstead was not a true harbor but a naturally formed inlet which offered protection near the shore. There was a constant bustle of ships, of seamen raising or lowering sails, or rowing their galleys swiftly through the waters. There were hundreds of canal boats always on the river transporting bales of merchandise or sacks of grain or cotton, where they would be unloaded at the piers and transferred to the many warehouses and granaries.

"Have you ever seen the like, Dr. Watson?" Whittingham exclaimed, his eyes darting here and there. Never had he seen so many people or such a bustling array of activities.

"No, Whittingham, it sure is a sight to see. I don't believe I have ever seen so many ships and such a diversity of them," Watson replied.

"It is like a magical place; people and shops everywhere. Look, dogs, goats, chickens and camels! I have never seen a camel!" exclaimed Whittingham. "And everyone just seems to be happy and content. They all get together and sing when they work. Do you hear them?"

Watson looked upon the people mingling about, children tugging ropes tethered to goats or donkeys, women carrying baskets of fruits, breads and more upon their heads in earthenware pots or reed woven baskets. Above the din of the constant chatter was the feeling of serene calmness, of a culture of people at peace not only with their land but with each other.

"I see what you mean, boy. There is a sense of peace here."

"I like it, Dr. Watson. I like this place called Egypt," Whittingham grinned.

"As do I, my boy, as do I."

At the roadstead, they boarded a small canal boat that took them the short distance to the paddle steamer *Queen's Traveler*. They stepped to the narrow jetty and Minnie Rothman protested, "I simply do not think I can board another ship!"

"I'm afraid you must. The *Queen's Traveler*," Princeton pointed out, "will be the last vehicle of water conveyance we will see for quite some time. Once we depart at Dashur, we will be on our own. Travel there is done mostly by walking or by donkey cart."

"What do you mean, Father?" Sharrey inquired. "I thought we would be staying in Cairo."

"No my dear, Cairo is far too great a distance for me to travel for my digs. We have set up several tents, one of which has been set exclusively for you and your friend. Another we must assign to Mr. Holmes and Dr. Watson. The boy will have to share quarters with the other servants and I had not thought of another lodger, Colter, I am sorry."

"No need to apologize, Professor. I am sure we will think of something. I may be able to share quarters with James. After all, I cannot think he would mind."

"No, not at all, but as I recall, there was a bit of mischief you two always managed to find."

"Yes, sir. We had many exciting times together, James and I," Colter replied. "You would not remember those times or me, Miss Princeton, as you were merely a babe. Allow me to introduce myself, albeit a bit late. My name is Colter Mitanni. I grew up here in Egypt and it was your father, as well as mine, that actually got me interested in archeology. James and I spent many hours on the digs, no wonder our interest."

"You and James are friends, then?" Sharrey asked.

"Yes we are, although we have been out of touch for some time. I have just completed my work at the dig outside of Alexandria while James has been busy assisting your father with his dig near the Red Pyramid in Dashur. I would have very much liked to join them there but I had already contracted my services elsewhere. Once that funding ran out, well, I guess I found myself with plenty of time. It was a bit of luck running into you both in Alexandria."

Holmes and Watson were behind Princeton, the women with Mitanni at his side. They were quiet, and Holmes was paying close attention to their conversation. At Mitanni's last remark, he glanced over to Watson, but Watson was distracted by the bustle about him. He made a mental note to speak with him later.

"Ah, here we are. I will check with the captain about accommodating everyone," Princeton said and stepped aboard the steamer. They waited while the heat was soaring and reaching sweltering heights. It was but a few minutes that he returned shaking his head. "I do apologize. The ladies will have to share a cabin, and Dr. Watson and Mr. Holmes will share a cabin. Colter, you can share mine with me. I am afraid the boy and Berihun will have to share quarters with the animals."

"The animals!" Minnie cried.

"It is all right, my dear. The animals are kept in open stalls and there is plenty of hay to keep them as well as Berihun and the boy warm at night. Quickly now we leave in minutes. The captain wishes to set sail before the zenith for it is soon that the dock workers stop for the afternoon. All must be loaded and we must be on board else we shall be left behind."

The *Queen's Traveler* was a large paddle steamer which carried mostly cargo and a few passengers. There were four private rooms that were for travelers' accommodations. The rest of the ship was loaded with bales of wheat, hay and grains, stalls filled with horses, camels, goats, sheep, chickens and donkeys. Whittingham left the group and the bags on deck and rushed to the open stalls. He passed the horses and the stall filled with cages of squawking chickens of various colors. He came to a stop at the stall where eight small donkeys were tethered. He reached out to touch the face of a small gray donkey, the tip of one ear missing. It warmed to his touch and drew forward to poke its muzzle into Whittingham's chest and nibbled at his shirt.

"One must be cautious for these little beasts will eat anything," Berihun said, coming up behind Whittingham.

"Really? He would eat my shirt?"

Berihun laughed. "No, young one, it is not your shirt he is interested in. I believe it is the spot of honey that was dropped from your breakfast toast."

"Oh!" Whittingham laughed. "I like these little fellows."

"These 'little fellows' as you call them, are the life of Egypt. They carry goods as well as people. They are sure footed and sound and do not require much. They are very stubborn and self-willed, but when one gives his love and trust to a human, he will become his best friend forever. Owning one of those little fellows is a mark of a prosperous merchant."

"I wish I had one. Someday, Berihun, I will be prosperous and own one of these; perhaps more than one." Whittingham smiled and rubbed the donkey's ears and the animal closed his eyes, resting his fuzzy stubbled chin against Whittingham's shoulder. "Perhaps I shall buy this one. He does seem to like me. I will call him Stubble because his chin is hairy and prickly."

"I think, young one, a new name might be in order. This one is a female and may have cause to dislike the name of Stubble."

Whittingham laughed. "All right then, I shall call her Queenie, after this boat. What do you say to that, Berihun?"

"Queenie. Yes that is a fine name for she is a fine animal."

"Are you two deciding on your quarters?" Watson queried. "If you are done, would you be so kind as to help the rest of us with the luggage?"

"Beg your pardon, sir. I did not mean to be neglectful," Whittingham hugged the little donkey then rushed over, and with Berihun, soon had the bags and trunks deposited

"Young one?" Berihun called to Whittingham from his new post at Sharrey's door. "Make our lodging arrangements with Queenie and we shall bed there."

"Great!" Whittingham grinned. "But first I must stop and see the camels."

"Take great care with the camel, young one, for they are not as loving nor forgiving as the donkey and their bite is as bad as their kick. Remain cautious about them," Berihun said and Whittingham rushed back to the stalls.

Chapter Ten

Princeton's room was beside his daughter's with Holmes and Watson across from that. The room next to them was occupied by another passenger; one they never set eyes on during their trip from Alexandria to Dashur.

"At least we have the courtesy of two small beds, eh Holmes." Watson tossed his bag onto the sagging thing that was called a bed.

"It makes no never mind, Watson. We will be taking turns with the door open keeping an eye on the hall. And keep your voice down."

"But Berihun is always there."

"Yes, but is that enough? Don't you find it strange the manner in which Professor Princeton greeted his daughter and his profession of the danger that lurks about? Not to mention how odd that Colter Mitanni would happen about? What do you make of the man?"

"He appears to be well enough. Apparently he is good friends with the Professor and James. And he is in the archeological field and in Egypt, making it believable that it was a coincidental encounter."

"I do not believe in coincidence, Watson. He has already made an error. You did not notice?" Watson shook his head. "When we were at the *Sunda I* he appeared to not know the dig site of Professor Princeton, yet when he introduced himself to Miss Princeton, he stated with certainty where he had been working and that Professor Princeton's dig site was at Dashur, at the Red

Pyramid specifically. This was not mentioned by the professor, as you will recall.

"And there is the matter of the other passenger in the next room of whom we know nothing about, either whether it be man or woman. We shall keep our conversations at a whisper, lest whoever it is happens to be eavesdropping through the wall. These Egyptians all seem to dress alike making it extremely difficult to tell one from the other."

"I agree and I am grateful for your advice and laid out the purchase of a pair of white trousers and tunic. I believe they will fare much better in this environment than our London tweeds."

"Well enough I dare say. If you don't mind, Watson, I am going to walk about the steamer. I will return shortly. By the way," Holmes paused at the door, "for the remainder of the journey, do not be evident in our quest to protect Miss Princeton for I fear our involvement will only increase her danger."

"I do not understand, Holmes…"

"I had the distinct impression from Professor Princeton that our presence here is entirely unwanted. Something is amiss here…something very dangerous and although his daughter is in the center of that danger, he was very keen for us to be out of the way. He declared she was in danger, yet never did reveal what the danger was. We shall remain on guard and be watchful over her safety, but we shall be discreet with our investigations."

"As you wish," Watson replied.

Holmes cocked his head. A finger to his lips hushed Watson. Throwing the door open he found Whittingham, his hand raised to tap the door.

"So sorry, sir, but Captain Ansari wishes to inform everyone that they prepare a meal around seven."

"Thank you, Whittingham. Please inform the others. Are you faring all right?"

"Right enough, sir. This land, sir, is the most amazing magical place I have ever seen, sir. Thank you for keeping me on."

"You're welcome. Now off with you. Be back shortly, Watson."

It was several hours yet before all the animals and cargo were loaded. Tethering the last of the camels, one of the workers nodded to the captain who then gave orders for the ship to be under way. The *Queen's Traveler* gave a slight shift when the steam pulsed through her core, giving life to the paddles. With a puff of smoke, the horn sounded signaling her departure. Once in the clear the captain set the paddles in motion. Smooth and effortless, the floats slapped the water one by one thrusting the steamer forward and she steered towards the center of the Nile.

Captain Ansari was a seasoned seaman and despite the crowded waters of the Nile, deftly maneuvered the steamer through the tangle of incoming and outgoing crafts. They'd gotten a late start and it was some time before the lights of Alexandria faded in the distance.

Sharrey stared at her bed, her traveling bag near the foot. She sat down and sighed, tired from the long day. The evening meal had been hastily prepared and just as hastily eaten. Everyone retired early.

"I can't believe we are finally under way, Minnie. It shan't be long now. Father says two maybe three days and we will be in Dashur."

"I can hardly wait. Sailing is not for me, although I must admit, I am very happy that I came." Minnie was at the basin of water.

"Yes, there's so much going on! I can hardly believe this place. I do hope that now that this country has come under British rule they are allowed to just be themselves. There is such a diversity of culture here and what a wonderful ancient culture it is!" Sharrey exclaimed.

"I thought you were set against this barbaric land, Shar? After all, most of these people still live like barbarians. They seem to make no effort to push themselves into the nineteenth century and become civilized. Riding donkeys and camels, wearing robes instead of proper clothing, you understand what I mean?" Minnie asked. "Here, I saved you some clean water."

"Thanks, Minnie. You know, back in England, one becomes accustomed to the daily routine of a strict set of social standards not knowing or understanding that the standards set for one civilization do not necessarily mean they should be the same for every civilization. I like the whole carefree way these people go about their everyday lives. I like that they work hard and help each other and still believe in their heritage of old pharaohs and ancient gods." Sharrey wrung out the cloth and placed it on the sideboard near the wash basin.

"It is rather quaint, but I could never live here. Could you?" Minnie mumbled through the silk of a fresh gown slipping over her head.

Sharrey sat on the bed and thought for a moment. Minnie curled on the small bed opposite and asked once more, "Well? Could you?"

"It may be the Egyptian blood in me that is going to say yes, Minnie. Somehow, I feel this is where I belong;

where I should have grown up all my life. I do not know how to tell Father that I am going to stay for apparently he feels my life is in danger here and wishes to send me back."

"You made that decision in the short time you've been here?" Minnie asked. "But what about home? What about England?"

"What about it? What sort of life did I ever really have in England? I was always alone. If it had not been for you, my best friend, I would have no one, Minnie. I am tired of being alone. I am tired of having no one. There I was never truly English. I grew up there learning how to be a proper English woman but there was always something deep in my heart that insisted I did not belong there.

"But here, I feel that my mother's blood has rekindled itself in my veins and I can truly become the Egyptian I was meant to be. I know Father provided well for me, but what good is all the gold in the world if one is unhappy? What good is being a proper English woman if it makes you uncomfortable? All those teachings of what constitutes a civilized society and what constitutes a barbaric one are all thrown into the wind when it really comes down to who you really are. These people are not barbarians nor uncivilized, Minnie. They simply chose to keep in touch with their past, their heritage, live the simple life as long as all their wants and needs are met. There is nothing barbaric about that, Minnie. And this country, this Egypt! My Egypt for now I feel that here is where I belong. There is so much to see…so much to learn. Yes, I know this is where I belong. And I intend to stay."

"Not to mention that Colter Mitanni is something to see."

"All right, that is quite enough, my friend. I think we should try to get some rest despite this awful heat. Father says it cools down quite a bit at night so perhaps it won't be too horrible. Goodnight, Minnie." Sharrey blew out her lamp.

"Goodnight, Shar. And …he really is handsome," Minnie giggled.

"The women have retired for the evening, Watson. I am much too restless to sleep so will stand the watch. I will wake you if there is anything untoward," Holmes said.

"Thank you, Holmes. I will try to get some rest despite these makeshift beds. At least we do have the privacy of our own room. Goodnight, Holmes," Watson said.

"Goodnight, Watson," Holmes returned. There really was no need for him to stand watch for Berihun was posted, as usual, outside Miss Princeton's door. He took the time to study the man, his keen eyes swept over the tall, muscular man. There was a loyal man willing to die if necessary to protect his charge. He was a man who spoke very little yet absorbed everything around him.

Berihun shifted his gaze to meet the gray-blue scrutinizing stare of Holmes. For several seconds it seemed they studied each other until Holmes acquiesced with a curt nod then closed his door. Sharrey Princeton would be well protected that night.

"The evening cooled nicely, don't you think Shar?" Minnie threw her coverlet back and stretched.

"Yes, it was a comfortable night despite the awful bed," Sharrey replied. She poured two steaming hot cups of tea and reached for a chunk of bread from the tray newly delivered. "This is strange bread. A little plain and bland but I suppose that is how they make it here."

"There are a lot of strange things here in case you hadn't noticed, Shar."

"This is true. Father said the journey to Cairo was the longest part of the journey and we should be arriving there before nightfall."

"I imagine there would be all sorts of things to see. It is very unfortunate we are stopping only long enough to deliver supplies. I would like to visit some of those temples I hear people talk about," Minnie said.

"Speaking of which," Sharrey quickly changed her clothes.

"Speaking of what?"

"It is a pity we missed so much during the night but I intend to see as much as I can along the way. I know it is going to get abominably hot out there, but I am going up on deck and see the sights. I would love to stop at all these new and interesting places, too, but Father says we must get back. It is a pity. Perhaps when James has recovered, he can be our guide and show us the real Egypt."

"I would like that, Shar. But, if you do not mind, I will say here and read. Don't forget your parasol. That sun is treacherous out there."

"Yes, thank you. I will be back soon." Sharrey left and Berihun followed her to the deck where she strolled leisurely about. Her original dislike of having Berihun always following her had been replaced with a grateful acceptance since the incident on the *Sunda I*.

She took great care to keep within the shade, her parasol twirling above her. She caught sight of Colter

Mitanni standing near the rails and watched as the breeze rumpled his dark hair, his hat cocked to one side, his bronzed skin even darker in the Egyptian sun. Her breath caught in her throat and her step faltered. Foolish girl, she thought, but her heart raced once more when he turned at her approach.

"I see you have taken quite an interest in our Egypt," Mitanni said.

"Yes, it is so lovely, despite the heat and the sand," Sharrey said.

"It is the heat and the sand that make Egypt. You see if you look there," he slipped his arm in hers, "we have left Alexandria behind. We are traveling in the western branch of the Nile. The Nile is a great river that runs from south to north Africa beginning far away in the mountains. Once she reaches Lower Egypt, she breaks into the eastern and western branches. There you see we have just passed the city of Tanta on our right. You can barely see it, but off in the distance, it is there. It is one of the major cities where cotton is grown and cultivated. It will take some time before we reach the branch of the Nile where Cairo stands."

"I am glad I did not miss that. But why are we traveling so slow," Sharrey said.

"There is much traffic on the river and there are other ships, small crafts of the native people that dart to and fro; not to mention the wildlife and the heavy weight of all the cargo on board this steamer. The captain is very adept at steering clear of wildlife in the water. To hit something could be catastrophic not only for the animal involved but also for the steamer. To become grounded in the Nile is not a good thing.

"But see there. All along the banks, for you shall see soon, there will be hippopotamus and crocodiles hiding in the reeds. These you would wish to stay clear of as the crocodiles would have you for lunch and the hippos are extremely territorial and will fight to the death to defend their piece of the Nile. They are giant animals of wonder and incredulously strong and dangerous. But you will also see beauty. Look, there are herons and cranes and there, in between the reeds, you see the white egret. It is a great beauty that white egret. Its feathers are long and silky, prized for adornment, but is against the law of the ancient gods to hunt them down. They were a sacred bird of the old gods and remain so today. If one should kill the sacred bird, he would be condemned to a hellish existence in the afterlife. If one should find the feather of the great white egret, it is a sign of good luck and a long happy life."

"You seem to know a lot about the Nile," Sharrey said.

"It is my home. I was born and raised here and would not wish to be any place else. Oh, look, there is a herd of gazelle coming to the water. You see the one standing to the side? He is the watcher. He will drink after all have taken their fill. It is his duty to watch and alert the others to the signs of the crocodile. Sometimes the watcher is not so good and one is taken by the crocodile. But that is life along the Nile.

"Once we reach the fork where the river divides, we will enter into the great Mother Nile which courses throughout Africa. She will take us past the most wonderful sights our ancestors have created."

"I am interested in learning as much as I can about Egypt. My mother was Egyptian, as you know, and I feel as though I am finally connecting not only with her but

109

with a life I should have known and been a part of all along."

"I understand all you are saying, Miss Princeton," Mitanni said. "It is a pity we cannot visit Cairo, for I am sure you would love to walk through the ruins and touch Egypt under your feet, feel Egypt coursing through your blood and hear Egypt whispering in your mind. This is a wonderful land. It calls out to the spirit of any true Egyptian until you are brought home to it."

"I can hardly wait," Sharrey smiled warmly.

"I see Miss Princeton and Mitanni have spent the better part of this day together," Holmes said upon returning to the room.

"Oh? That is good news. She is safe there. I expect Berihun is not too far off."

"No, actually sitting at the donkey stall not far away with Whittingham."

"Good, then she is safe. I truthfully do not understand why anyone would want to be out in this searing heat but I gather the temperature is cooling now that dusk is on the horizon. I will be glad once we have unloaded our cargo at Cairo and back on our way. Our food is there, by the way," Watson indicated the tray on the small table. "I hope you do not mind, I have already eaten. I have covered yours with the linen as the flies are persistent here."

"Thank you, Watson. The captain assures me we should be in Dashur within two days if not sooner if all goes well. There are no stops after Cairo, so we need not worry about others coming on board." Holmes poured a cup of tepid tea and eyed it with distaste. "A brandy would do better than this tea."

"I daresay it would, Holmes, but we must keep our wits about us. Have you heard anything of Miss Rothman?"

"No, I take it she is still in her cabin?"

"She has been there all day. I saw a workman from the ship deliver a tray there just moments ago. I have kept watch but there is nothing amiss going on in the hall."

"Good man, Watson. Because we feel safe and secure aboard this boat does not mean we are. I am happy to see Berihun still keeping his charge. Whittingham appears to be getting along well with him."

"That boy is a natural no matter which environment we put him in. He has fallen in love with a small donkey, by the way. Calls her Queenie."

"He seems a fine lad," Holmes said stretching on the bed. "I think I will nap. Keep watch will you?"

"So, Cairo is your capital?" Sharrey asked once the trays were removed.

"Yes, Cairo is the largest city in Africa and a great political and religious center. It is so great, it spills to both banks of the Nile. Old Cairo is where the Giza Plateau is located and if you wait for just a few minutes, we shall see it on the other bank of the Nile, across from Greater Cairo. Here are built the great pyramids of the pharaohs on the Giza Strip as well as those built in Saqqara some distance further."

"The boat is slowing," Sharrey said.

"Yes, there are some items to unload then we will be back on our way. We are entering the busy shipping lanes of the Nile where boats and ships of all sorts travel between the Old Cairo of the Giza Strip and the Greater Cairo where the most recent inhabitants live. There is much trade here and even greater interest in the pyramids by visitors from other countries. All watercraft must slow and be watchful of even the smallest craft on the water for to upset even one could cause catastrophic results."

The *Queen's Traveler* slowed to a crawl, easing slowly into an open pier. There, most of the cargo of animals was unloaded, along with bales of hay and wheat. Mitanni pointed to the Giza Strip where Sharrey could see the tops of the three greatest pyramids of Egypt shrouded in a mist of Saharan dust.

"It is absolutely beautiful!" she said.

"Yes it is. And this is just the beginning. The wonders of Egypt are all about us, every day and everywhere. One must only look."

Several hours later, the steamer was once more inching through the bustling Nile waterways, several times forced to come to a stop to avoid a collision. A smattering of gray cloud crept into the sky. The hot afternoon gradually shifted into a hot sultry evening.

Mitanni walked Sharrey back to her room. Berihun took up his position once more. With their return, Watson lay down with a sigh of relief. His vigil was over.

Chapter Eleven

The crew of the *Queen's Traveler* was a meager crew, but they had clean tables and the evening meal prepared simply yet satisfying. Served after sunset were cooked chunks of goat's meat with large round portions of flat bread for dipping into the sauce. There was tea and coffee and the ever present tray of figs, dates and olives.

"I am ravenous!" Minnie Rothman exclaimed.

"As am I," said Sharrey. From where she sat, she surveyed the steamer, its remaining cargo of hay and wheat, its bleating of goats and sheep and the clucking of caged chickens. Her gaze wandered past Berihun standing near the camel stall, his ever present figure no longer an obstacle but a blessing. The brown flowing waters of the Nile blurred into the green fertile banks and the swaying of palm trees and marsh grasses shimmered with a myriad of colors.

"You know, with the incidents Father wrote in his letters, I was prepared to dislike this place called Egypt. But as I sit here and take in all the beauty, I cannot. It is a land of enchantment; a land of great rulers and exquisite monuments. They may not have lived as we live or believed as we believe, yet what they believe and how they live has withstood the ages of time. Their legacy and contribution to the world will never be forgotten."

"Why Miss Princeton," Mitanni said approaching the table, "you are quite the romantic."

"Not a romantic, Mr. Mitanni, a realist. I have grown up alone and have come to acquire a very realistic and pragmatic attitude. And London seems to condone that. But here, amidst all of this beauty, I believe I can toss a bit of that pragmatist aside."

"Ah, Professor," Mitanni rose "your daughter and I have been discussing the beauty of Egypt."

Princeton, Watson and Holmes sat down. "And that is as it should be. Her heritage is here. Do not forget Sharrey, your mother was an Egyptian. I beg your pardon," Princeton said to Minnie, apparently noticing her for the first time. "I do not recall your name."

"Oh, Father, this is Minerva Rothman. She is my best and dearest friend and I do hope you don't mind that I have asked her to accompany me," Sharrey said.

"Not at all, my dear. Minerva Rothman, eh? I once knew an Agnes Rothman; married a colleague of mine and partner in some of my digs. A Professor Benedict Rothman. Was he a relation?"

"Yes, sir," Minnie said. "Benedict Rothman was my father."

"Oh my! Why, I have not seen Agnes in years. You were such a small child at the time. It was such a shame. I mean about your father."

"What about my father?"

"Did not your mother tell you?" Princeton asked. Minnie shook her head and he continued. "Oh dear, I am sorry. But as I have opened this can of worms, I am afraid I must continue. It was back, oh eighteen years or so ago. I believe, my dear, you were just a tiny girl four or five at the time. Your father and I were on a dig in the Valley of the Kings. There was so much going on at the time. When archeology was about digging and finding treasures of monetary importance   and becoming famous. Not like today where we archeologists have pushed to preserve dig sites, find and preserve not only the physical treasures these generations left behind but also to find and preserve the heritage, the life styles and their religions, their culture and their beliefs. It is all a matter of archeology, now my dear.

"But back then, of course, things were different. People rushing about, workers carting off loads of sand, excavations being dug. We were young, careless, yes we were young. And excited, for not long before there had been some excitement over the discovery of a tomb. At least everyone thought it was a tomb. We rushed over to look and of course were immediately drawn into the excitement of the moment. Benedict and I jumped into the deep opening that the workers had excavated, why it was nearly ten feet down but in our enthusiasm it seemed like nothing. We reached for shovels and were vigorously working at removing the last few feet of sand blocking the entrance when the sand embankment gave way. The weight of all those workers had compromised the integrity you see. And down it came. Cascading like a waterfall and we could not stop it, climb over it or get above it.

"Soon Benedict and I were covered. I knew we were in danger and threw my shovel. I pulled my tunic over my head and curled into a ball, thus giving myself an air pocket, hopefully enough to sustain me until the workers could dig us out. Benedict was not so lucky. I was nearly dead but was rescued in time. Benedict died. When the sand collapsed, he apparently fell against the shovel and...well. It killed him. There was nothing we could do. Nothing we could have done. We were so young then. We were such fools then."

"Oh Father!" Sharrey whispered.

"His death, no matter the manner, grieves me greatly as he was my father, but I have no recollection of him. My mother simply told me he had died in Egypt. I hope you do not blame yourself, Professor, for I do not. It appears to have been a tragic accident." Minnie Rothman squeezed Princeton's hand.

"Yes it was, my dear, and I thank you for your kind words, but had we remained at our own site, it would never have happened, at least not to us. Had we allowed the workers to finish the excavation and shore up the opening, it would not have happened. And I fear, your mother blamed me. She was upset and angry, making accusations, unfounded and hurtful statements. She left Egypt after that. Returned to England. I lost tract of her then. How is she?"

"She is well, Professor, thank you for asking," Minnie replied.

"That is a tragic story, Professor," Watson said.

"Just so, but not long after that my Sharrey was born and I was involved with my children. My wife, Sari Nefrati, passed during childbirth, I...I could not bear the loss and that is why I traveled to London with Sharrey, leaving her there in the care of governess and nannies to educate her and keep her safe."

"Now, Professor, you have approached the subject of safety. It might be time for you to fill us in as to why you did not wish your daughter here," Holmes said.

"Yes, yes of course," Princeton hesitated, searching Sharrey's face. "You have her beauty, Sharrey, for Sari was a beauty. Her hair was black as the night and glistened like diamonds across dark waters in moonlight. She would wear it sometimes loose over her shoulders letting the evening wind catch it and blow it softly about her face. Her eyes were black also, great round eyes filled with love and laughter. You have my eyes, blue and piercing. But on you, there is a much greater beauty than I could ever possess," Princeton sighed. "I still remember her as if she were here now. Her beauty, her skin brown and smooth and smelling of the ancient galbanum oils of Egypt."

"I wish I had known her, Father."

"As do I, my dear. I met Sari when Benedict and I were working on the dig at Thebes. She was working at the Cairo museum and knew more about Egyptian antiquities than anyone I have ever known. We fell in love with her, both Benedict and I. Yet, as handsome as Benedict was, for he was truly a handsome lad, Minnie, Sari fell in love with me. Me! Of all people. I was the happiest man in the world and once I knew her heart, we married immediately. She had no family, no one. I became that someone. And within a year, James was born. I need not give you the particulars on that. It suffices to say that we were very much in love. She came with me to the digs, she assisted me at the digs, she was the love of my life and my best friend. A man could not be happier than that."

"What happened then, Father?"

"That was about the same time we met Agnes Pendergast. She was here on a holiday with other friends and got caught up in the archeological thrust of things. I could see her heart was for Benedict, though he pined over the loss of Sari to me. But Agnes's persistence paid off and soon they were married also. A wonderful couple. Agnes so adored him. That's why his death was so tragic."

"Are you telling me that James and I played together as children?" Minnie asked.

"Yes, of course. There was you and James and, of course, Colter here. You three were inseparable. Always getting into some sort of mischief. Strange after all these years you will all be together again, and no doubt there will be mischief once more," Princeton said.

"But I thought James was…"

"He is, my dear, but I am hoping that your lovely face will wake him from his coma."

"Is that why you sent me to England, Father? Because I reminded you of mother's death?" Sharrey asked.

"No! No! Not at all! I sent you to England for your own safety."

"Ah, now we come to the heart of the matter," Holmes said.

"Before I begin, I must have Berihun come. There is a tale he will tell you that you must know of before I can tell mine. It is a strange tale, but a true tale. Berihun! Come! It is time to tell them of Snefru and Amanirena."

Berihun approached the table warily. He knew the time would come when he would have to relate the story of Snefru and Amanirena. He also knew that anyone not of the ancient Egyptian descent would not understand. But before he could begin, Whittingham came stumbling towards them with a groan, clutching his head, the blood running freely through his fingers.

"Whittingham!" Watson shouted, reaching the boy first, catching him just as the boy crumpled to the deck. "Boy! What has happened?"

"Rooms!" was all the boy could mutter.

"Holmes! To our quarters!" Watson cried. He bent to scoop the boy in his arms.

"No, no, do not go there," Whittingham murmured. "There is danger. I went to check ...a noise there. I saw someone dressed in dark robes searching through your things. I surprised him but he saw me, he rushed upon me and hit me. When I fell, he ran from the room and I could not stop him. I am so sorry, sir," Whittingham moaned.

"See to the boy, Watson!" Holmes hurried towards the small cabin. The door stood ajar and Holmes approached cautiously. But there was no one to be seen. Their bags had been opened and their contents thrown about the floor and beds. Holmes knew exactly what they were searching for. Closing the door he returned to the deck where Watson and Berihun had taken Whittingham to their cloaks in the donkey stall. Watson had already washed and bandaged the wound and Whittingham lay quiet.

"How is the boy, Watson?" Holmes asked.

"He has a mild concussion, I think, but otherwise he will be all right. I must insist he stay here for at least the night. No food, only water. The concussion will bring the lad a frightful headache by morning and food will only make him vomit. Keep him quiet, Berihun. Holmes and I will see to Miss Princeton," Watson said.

"Of course," Berihun nodded.

"What of our cabin?" Watson asked.

"It is as the boy said. Our bags have been gone through and we have things to put to right, but otherwise no damage. We should accompany the ladies to their quarters and make sure things are safe there," Holmes said.

"You will get no argument from me," Minnie said. "Oh Sharrey, this is becoming too frightening. First the attack on you back on the *Sunda I* and now the attack on this poor boy, Whittingham!"

"There was an attack on the ship? Why was I not told of this?" Princeton demanded.

"It was in the past, Father, I am all right," Sharrey smiled at him.

"No, my dear, this is not acceptable. You must tell me what happened!"

"Someone managed to get a cobra on board and put it in your daughter's room, Professor. It would have killed her if Berihun not had his wits about him," Watson said.

"A cobra? Oh lord! This is certainly getting out of hand," Princeton groaned.

"You know, once when James visited us back in England, he told us silly stories of curses and things and we just laughed at him," Sharrey said with a shudder. "But I am beginning to think those stories of curses are no laughing matter."

"No, no," Princeton said. "They are no laughing matter. There are forces in Egypt that we do not know anything of. Their culture is far older than anything we could possibly imagine. It predates the dark ages and the middle ages and the ages of the old gods and magic of worlds into the eons of time that have been forgotten by any mortal. These people are the ancients. Descended from time out of mind and no one actually knows for sure what powers they hold."

"Father, you are scaring us!" Sharrey cried. "Surely you speak of fictional superstitions!"

"I do not wish to frighten you, my dear, but there are mysteries in this land that have been hidden for such a long time. Mysteries that cannot be explained." The dark gravity of Princeton's voice frightened them all.

"Mr. Princeton," Holmes said, "why don't we make sure the ladies are safe within their cabin. Watson and I will be on watch. You may be sure they will be safe."

"Thank you, Mr. Holmes. Minnie and I are grateful for your presence here. I know now that having you accompany us was the smartest decision I have ever made."

Back in their room, Watson was refolding the clothes that had been strewn about. "So much for keeping a low profile, eh Holmes? What do you make of this incident?"

"They were after the ring and the box once more, Watson. It all makes sense now beginning with bumping into you on the *Sunda I*, the cobra in Miss Princeton's room, and now this. They, whoever they are, are eliminating possibilities of where the ring and the box are. There final conclusion will be that I or Miss Princeton has them on our person. There is no other explanation. We must be on our guard for now the stakes are greater, the game has escalated."

"But what fools they are to believe we would not secretly exchange the location of the items."

"That is true." Holmes tapped the small package in his breast pocket. Not once since they had begun their voyage had he felt the items there were in danger of being taken from him. They were safe there. "My first and foremost concern is Miss Princeton."

"I, too, am becoming increasingly concerned as this case moves forward. First the attempt with that snake and now this! To attack a mere boy! Whoever it is, he is becoming desperate to obtain that box, Holmes."

"Yes, and it is apparent he will stop at nothing to get it."

"The attack does settle one risen question. It could not have been Miss Rothman. She was with us the entire time and appeared genuinely shocked at the attack on the boy."

"Yes, that is true. It could also eliminate Colter Mitanni from suspicion as he was in our company also. But, that does not eliminate the fact that either Mitanni or Rothman could have arranged the breakin just for that purpose, thereby diverting suspicion from themselves."

"I had not thought of that, Holmes. So we are back to the beginning. As you said, trust no one, suspect everyone."

"I am afraid so. We are no further ahead on this case then when we began other than that our objective has changed."

"Objective?"

"Yes. Miss Princeton hired us to accompany her to Egypt and bring her father and brother back home to England with her. But we have stepped into a case much more diabolical for it includes danger and murder and it has nothing to do with curses. Every corner we turn adds more to the suspects and less to the actual perpetrator. And of course, there is still the why of it. First watch or second?"

"I'll take the first watch as I am already at the door. Try to get some rest. I will wake you in a few hours, Holmes."

"Very good," Holmes said easing his tall frame onto the bed. Watson pulled the door open several inches more and positioned a chair against the wall there. Sitting sideways with one foot nudging the door back and forth, he had a clear view of Sharrey Princeton's room just a few feet down the hall.

Some minutes passed before Holmes spoke. "I have been thinking, Watson."

"Yes?"

"I have been thinking that it is nearly impossible to close my eyes and get any rest while you are playing with that squeaking door."

"I apologize, Holmes, old man. It was entirely unconscious on my part. I have been staring at Miss Princeton's door and going over the past several weeks."

"About anything in particular?"

"Just think about this, Holmes," Watson removed his foot from the door. "Miss Princeton receives the ring and the box from her father. She has the thing in her possession for more than a week and nothing is amiss. It is only after she decides to go to Egypt that these strange events began to occur. Why then?"

"That's a good point, Watson," Holmes sat up and leaned back, searching for his pipe. After lighting and taking several puffs, he blew the gray smoke upward and leaned back with his eyes closed, breathing in its last floating remnants, as if it were the smoke that incited thought. "You are correct. We must ask Miss Princeton what exactly prompted her to decide to go to Egypt."

"Ah, we may be able to do so now. I see a light has just appeared under her door. Perhaps we should check?"

"Allow me." Holmes went down the hall to Sharrey's door and knocked lightly. A few moments later she whispered, "Who is it?"

"Holmes, Miss Princeton. I saw the light and wondered if everything was all right."

Sharrey undid the latch, opened the door slowly and stepped out. "I could not sleep but did not wish to disturb Minnie."

"In that case, would you mind coming to our room. There are some questions we would like to ask?"

"No, not at all." Sharrey drew her shawl over her dressing gown. She entered Holmes's room and Watson rose quickly and offered her the chair. "If you don't mind, I will sit just here. As unseemingly a bed as it is, it is more comfortable than that chair," she said, noting the sagging rattan center.

"Of course," Watson replied.

"Now then, what is it that you wished to ask?"

"We shall keep our voices low, Miss Princeton. We do not know who is in the next room to us," Holmes indicated with a slight nod "Before you came to us at Baker Street, how long had you had the ring and the box in your possession?"

"It was nearly two weeks. As I said, when I tried it on, I was overtaken with that strange sensation and so decided to put the thing out of sight and try not to think about it."

"Really," Holmes mused. "Then after two weeks, what changed your mind that caused you to decide to go to Egypt?"

"I…I believe it was the letter from Father," she said.

"It does not take a consulting detective to see that your relationship with your father is somewhat strained. Considering a journey of this magnitude…"

"I understand what you are saying, Mr. Holmes," Sharrey interrupted him, "and believe me, I wish that were not so. My father has, in all appearance, cast me aside only fulfilling those obligations he feels are a necessity as a father. But deep down, down there in that cold heart of his somewhere, Mr. Holmes, I have to believe he really does love me. I…it is difficult for me to admit this, but I have spent my entire life waiting and longing for his visits. I would say and do whatever he wished, whatever I thought would make him happy for I so desperately wished to see it in his eyes, feel it through his touch. But he kept such a distance from me.

"Owing to all of that, Mr. Holmes, I love my father very much. I would still, to this day, say or do whatever he wishes of me if only he would give me that one spark of a touch, or a look, that tells me he loves me as much as I love him. It was this that weighed heavy on me when I received his letter.

"I was in such a dark mood, that when Minnie came to visit I finally lost my composure in all of this and broke down and confessed all to her. I told her of my father and his distancing himself from me, of my love for him and my concern for his safety and welfare. I showed her Father's letter and she asked to see the ring.

"She of course, immediately fell in love with the ring and tried it on and I would have gladly given it to her for I abhor the thing for what it does to me. But Berihun was there and when I saw the look upon his face when Minnie put the ring on her finger, I felt fear for my life. Oh! No, no, he did not say a word or make a move, but his eyes said all that needed to be said. I had Minnie put the ring back in the box and she read the letter. It was Minnie who insisted that I come to Egypt. She said my father would surely understand my reason for coming and see the love in my heart and would understand how I have felt all these years without him. I believed her. I wanted to believe her. I convinced myself that she was correct and that I really should do all I could to help my father and James, and when she insisted on accompanying me as my traveling companion so I would not be alone in my quest, well, then the idea was settled."

"So it was Miss Rothman who talked you into coming to Egypt?" Watson asked.

"Yes, in a way, but I know that sooner or later I would have made that decision myself. It was only Minnie who pushed the issue, insisting on the urgency of the matter considering James's condition and my father's fear staring up at me through the words of his letter."

"How long have you and Miss Rothman been friends?" Holmes asked.

"I have known Minnie for nearly ten years, Mr. Holmes, since her mother married Thaddeous Winston Carmichael. Once his father, the late Lord Brantwood Phillip Carmichael had passed, Thaddeous inherited his estate and the title, thereby becoming the next in line of the great Carmichael lords. They moved into the Carmichael manor not two miles from me and it was apparent that two girls so close in age and swiftly becoming friends should share tutors. Minnie came every day to my classroom. She is as close to me as a sister can possibly be and I would trust her with my life, Mr. Holmes."

Holmes cast a wary glance to Watson. "Thaddeous Carmichael. His wife would not be Agnes?"

"Yes, yes it is. She has been wonderful to me..." Sharrey stopped speaking when footsteps were heard in the hall. "I am sorry. It is getting late and I fear that if I am seen in the quarters of two gentlemen, it would scar my reputation." She quickly stepped into the hall. "Mr. Holmes, I do hope you get to the bottom of these attacks.

I will tell you once again, I am much relieved that you and Dr. Watson are with me on this voyage. Goodnight."

Holmes watched until he heard the lock slide home. Turning to Watson he said, "Agnes Carmichael. Well, well, well. Some of the pieces of the puzzle are coming together, Watson." Holmes seated himself in the chair by the door.

"In what way."

"That day at the museum. There was a woman viewing the recently acquired objects from Egypt when Sterling Jasper, the museum curator and I, went in to pay a visit to Professor Simpkins. Jasper pointed her out to me saying she was an avid collector of Egyptian artifacts and that her name was Mrs. Agnes Carmichael."

"Minnie Rothman? Do you suppose?"

"I am not merely supposing, my good man, I am believing. Agnes Pendergast meets and marries Benedict Rothman, who himself is in love with Sari Nefrati who has fallen in love and marries Peter Princeton. Both of which Peter Princeton and Benedict Rothman are partners in a dig down here in Egypt. Rothman and Princeton are involved in a tragic accident of which one of them dies; Rothman. Agnes Pendergast, now Rothman, has a child, Minerva, and she moves back to England, where she meets and marries Thaddeous Carmichael who becomes Lord of the manor within walking distance to the daughter of Peter Princeton. The daughter, Minerva Rothman and the daughter, Sharrey Princeton become friends, nearly sisters…"

"Minerva Rothman's mother is a collector of Egyptian antiquities and Sharrey Princeton's father is an archeologist of Egyptian antiquities. The two men who love the same woman, one winning her heart, the other marries another on a fallen lovers rebound, the tragic death, love, loss, passion and pain. Could this be a vendetta and not a curse?" Watson finished.

Holmes's eyebrows arched suspiciously. "Oh what a terrible tangled web we weave, eh Watson?"

Chapter Twelve

The *Queen's Traveler* paddled through the darkness leaving Cairo fading behind. The attack on Whittingham, a mere boy, left everyone with a feeling of dread and foreboding. This was the second attack on the Princeton party of travelers and it was beginning to look as though the curses of ancient pharaohs were something real and one such curse had attached itself to them.

The weather brought about a mist that settled across the Nile, one which was strange and unfamiliar to Egypt. That coupled with the fear of the recent attack kept the travelers closeted in their cabins for most of the day. Whittingham, his head bound in bandaging, once more relayed the message that a meager meal would be served on the deck.

"Dr. Watson, you frightened me!"Whittingham cried when Watson pulled the door open just as he was about to knock.

"Sorry, lad, I imagine you are a bit jumpy after yesterday. How is that head of yours?"

The boy pressed his head and grinned. "Doing fine, sir. You are a good doctor. Hardly hurts much at all. Course, my mum always said I had a thick skull."

Watson laughed and put an arm about the boy's shoulders. "Let us eat. I see the others have already gone. Holmes is about somewhere. What's on the menu this morning, young man?"

The boy laughed. "You know, Dr. Watson, the menu never changes, it is the same as always. I am glad we will be arriving in that city, what is it called?"

"Dashur."

"Yes, that Dashur city. Maybe the menu will change then," Whittingham smiled.

The others were already seated when Watson appeared. Princeton looked up. "Where is Holmes?"

"I do not know. I thought he was already here," Watson replied. "But let us not hold up the meal for him. Holmes is an odd sort. Wherever he is and whatever he is doing, he will arrive on his own accord and eat when he feels the need."

"Tomorrow we arrive at Dashur, Professor?" Minnie asked.

"Yes, it is an amazing city."

"I thought you said we would be staying at the dig site, Father," Sharrey said.

"We will, but Dashur is a city that is situated just several miles away from the dig site. The city itself has quite a number of families living there, some small shops, a clinic of sorts, vending stalls and a small inn or two. There is a well-traveled road that leads from my site to the city but it is much faster to travel by water using one of the small boats or barges always on hand."

"An inn? Then why are we staying at the site in tents?" Minnie exclaimed.

"You are not required to stay at the site, Miss Rothman," Princeton said. "I merely thought you might like to stay with the rest of the party and be able to visit with James. He is hospitalized in one of the tents there. In his condition, it did not matter where he was taken care of. We can fulfill his needs as well as the small clinic at Dashur."

"It's up to you, Minnie, but I am going to stay at the site with Father and James," Sharrey said.

"Of course, the site it is, for I will be happy to finally be on solid ground again!"

"I agree," Sharrey said. "This has been a long voyage, one of ships and fright. Once we settle in at the site I am sure things will return to normal, right Father?"

"That they should, my dear."

"You never did explain about the past…ah, Holmes," Watson exclaimed. "You are late and the meal merely remnants."

"No matter. I have been about the steamer and talking with the captain. We will be arriving at Dashur by late this evening. It appears he made up some time during the evening hours."

"We will not arrive in Dashur, Mr. Holmes, but several miles beyond it. The captain will dock near the dig site and we will disembark. He will then turn the steamer to Dashur. I suggest that everyone make their decision tonight where they wish to stay. Travel to the city is done on a need to basis. We generally stay at the site only traveling to Dashur for supplies; once a week is usually sufficient."

"That's interesting to note," Holmes said.

"I for one will be staying at the site with Father and James. Minnie has agreed also. And you, Mr. Mitanni?"

"At the site, there is no question. I am an archeologist heart and soul and would not miss the opportunity to lend a hand, if you would have me, Professor?"

"I would like that very much. With James incapacitated, we are behind our expected schedule and with my taking this week to go to Alexandria and escort you all back here I am afraid we are very far behind expectations. And on that note, if you will excuse me, I have things to do. Tomorrow will be a very busy day." Princeton rose abruptly and left.

"He may be right," Minnie said. "I think I will return to our room."

"I shall accompany you if you don't mind?" Watson said rising with her.

"Thank you, that is most appreciated," she said taking Watson's offered arm.

"If you two will excuse me," Holmes rose. He went far enough to be out of sight then remained hidden where he could observe Colter and Sharrey. The history of Agnes Carmichael and her possible quest for vengeance against Peter Princeton after all these years did not deter his suspicion against Colter Mitanni. There was no proof against Agnes Carmichael, and suspects were open.

Left alone together, an awkward moment lengthened until Sharrey rose and went to the rail. "I'm glad the mist cleared. The sunrise is beautiful here. I have never seen anything quite like this back in England."

"You never will," Colter said joining her. "The sunrise here is like no other in all the world. A great yellow disk rising rapidly in the east, pouring beams of brilliant yellow light upon the foliage and radiating sparkling diamonds in the water. In ancient Egyptian belief, the sun is the giver of life, revered as Ra the Sun God, rising each morning to renew life each day."

"You make the old ways sound like a magical time."

"You are quite the romantic, Miss Princeton," Colter smiled.

"Sharrey, please. I feel that we have known each other all of our lives although we have only just met. Your knowing my father and Minnie makes me feel just a bit envious."

"There is nothing to be envious about. My parents, your parents and Minnie's parents were all friends and members of the same archeological digs here in Egypt. The only difference was that my father and your mother were true Egyptians."

Sharrey turned with a puzzled look. "And knowing that, how did you ever come by the name of Colter?"

"Ah, you laugh at an Egyptian named Colter. Truth be told, I am rather proud of that name. My mother, Lucy Whitmore, was on holiday here and met my father, Mahmet Mitanni, one of Egypt's leading archeologists of that time. She was from America, the state of Montana. Out there it is called the wild west and she was one proud and tough woman. When I was born she suggested Colter to my father. He frowned at the name, but he loved my mother very much and gave in to her."

"That surprises me. You would think he would have insisted on an Egyptian name."

"You did not know my mother!" Colter laughed. "She was a most formidable woman and determined to have her way. Besides, my father loved her very much. I know there is the belief here that the man rules the family, and in some respects that is true. For this culture, it is good. It works for them. But my father and mother were so diverse in their cultures, that when they married they agreed to be considerate of each other's cultures and beliefs. It worked well for them."

"I wonder how that worked for my parents."

"Your parents were equally diverse in their cultures but theirs was a different relationship. Where your mother was a true Egyptian, your father wanted to be. He felt more at home here than anywhere else in the world and he loved your mother so much that whatever she wished for, he gave it to her. He denied her nothing, Sharrey. His love for her was so strong that when she died, a part of him died also. He was devastated. Didn't eat or sleep for days on end. Talked endlessly about the future of Egypt; of your future and how he had to protect you from that. Everyone thought he had lost his mind and suggested he take a respite from the dig and return to England.

"Despite the fact that he hadn't been to England in nearly ten years, he took you and James back to England then, but quickly returned only with James. He spoke to no one about his reasons why and everyone felt Peter Princeton had lost a part of his mind when he lost your mother. He loved her that much. It was only three days before your birth that Benedict Rothman had been killed in that cave in. And then, the day of your birth, your mother died. It was all so very tragic. It was not long after that the friends parted ways. There was just too much sadness and loss, torn friendships and lost loves."

"Oh how awful! No wonder my father is so distant."

"Yes, I have been privileged to have known a truly loving family."

"Tell me about them, Colter. I would like to hear something of happy news."

"My father was an archeologist and my mother loved him. She followed him from site to site and became his most valuable assistant. I, of course, was dragged along. Not only did I find it interesting, I loved it! I imagine now it was because of my Egyptian heritage but back then I was a child growing up and every site was a new adventure for me. You cannot imagine the life of a child growing up playing games between the great pillars of Karnak, swimming in the Nile with dangerous crocodiles on the far shore dreaming of having you for lunch, or falling from a camel traversing through the desert of miles upon miles of sand dunes where no water is to be found. It was a childhood of love, danger, adventure, knowledge and security. I would not have traded my childhood for anything."

"And where are your parents now?"

"They are both dead. I was seventeen when a stone pillar collapsed near Karnak. Both my parents were killed."

"Oh, Colter, I am so sorry."

"Do not be for they were so in love and they did everything together. It seemed fitting to have happened there for I believe they have been sent to the afterlife together. I would not have wished their passing any other way. I take great consolation that they are together. They are happy, I am sure of it."

"I like that," Sharrey said. "I like this Egyptian belief in the afterlife. It seems to make living here more tolerable knowing that somewhere out there, there is another place to continue your existence. Like there is more to life than we can ever imagine."

"Yes you do know that to the Egyptian there really is no death. Death is only the beginning."

"I like that."

"I like you, Sharrey. I know I have only just met you, but it seems that I have known you and waited for you all my life." Colter brushed the hair from Sharrey's eyes.

"And I like you too, Colter. And, strange as that sounds, I feel the same way." Colter bent to kiss her lightly on her cheek. "Perhaps when this is all over, when James is better and we settle this mystery at the dig site…perhaps."

"Yes, perhaps," Colter said, his gaze wandered across the Nile. "It is a shame we spent the evening in the dark. We missed the lights of Heliopsis and Saqqara but we should be coming upon Dashur before nightfall. The captain has made good time."

"I can hardly wait to visit with James this evening!" Sharrey exclaimed. "I should return to Minnie and repack my bags. I wish to be prepared. I can't wait to see my father at work and try to understand what is so thrilling and exciting about digging in sand, swallowing dust and burning in the hot sun. Then perhaps I will better understand why he did what he did all those years ago leaving me alone in England."

"I understand, for I, too, get that thrill of excitement every time I enter a dig site. The prospect of a new discovery is what drives every archeologist forward even at the expense of family and safety. I am afraid it is a fact of life for us. We single-minded men do not intend any neglect in that regard, it simply happens. You see, it is the thrill of the find, the driving force that pushes us to dig deeper, to move forward into ancient discoveries, into the darkened depths of narrow passageways, into…..," he stopped when Sharrey placed a hand over his mouth.

"Enough! I get it! So what you are telling me is that I should expect a life of neglect?"

Colter looked up sharp, taken aback by her statement. "If you are referring to me, I should say never. I can truly say what I feel for you Sharrey, is akin to that of your father for your mother and I would make you a promise here and now, that you will never be neglected again. But then, I apologize, I am out of line. I am making an assumption and have no right."

"Perhaps, Colter, perhaps not. But I will go now before anything else untoward will be said." She left him standing near the rail wondering.

Chapter Thirteen

The steamer gave a jolt, lurching to a complete stop. From everywhere came the shouting and cries of the captain and the crew rushing in all directions at once. Colter picked himself up, reaching for Sharrey. "Are you all right?"

"Yes, I am, but what happened?"

"That is what we would all like to know!" Watson and Holmes appeared along with Minnie and Professor Princeton.

"It is nothing," the captain shouted to them. "Something caught in one of the paddles. We must take care of it. It may be hours before we continue so I suggest that you all return to your cabins and let us go about our business."

"Oh no, this means we will not be arriving in Dashur tonight?" Minnie moaned.

"Most likely not my dear," Princeton said.

"I was looking forward to visiting with James," Sharrey said.

"Tomorrow is soon enough, my girl. Let us do what the good captain says and return to our cabins. There is not much we can do. These men are seasoned and will have us on our way soon."

Could this be another attempt to gain control of the ring and the box? Was this sabotage or merely an accident? Holmes's eyes swept the area, relieved when Berihun followed the women back to their quarters. He knew their safety was assured and he waited for them to leave. The captain had already ordered his men into the water by the time he and Watson joined them to examine the paddles that were now motionless. Three men were preparing to enter the water while four others arrived with weapons.

"What do you suppose that is about, Dr. Watson?" Whittingham asked.

"Boy! What are you still doing here? This is no place for a boy!" Watson exclaimed.

"Allow him to stay, Watson. He is a boy soon to be a man and he must learn all there is to learn about life. The divers are going into the water to determine why the paddles have stopped. There is something jamming them. The others will keep watch, two on each side of the boat for crocodiles or other predators that should happen into the water and threaten their shipmates," Holmes said.

"Would they really shoot at the predator and kill him?" Whittingham asked.

"They must, Whittingham. Crocodiles are a predator that will search and devour anything of flesh that is in the water. They show no mercy. There are also water snakes that if a person is bitten, one dies instantly a most horrifically painful death, not to mention the threat from the hippopotamus, an animal extremely territorially protective. The waters of the Nile may be beautiful, but they are also dangerous to the unsuspecting. Now watch."

Once the shooters were in place the three divers took to the water. Gripping the paddles of the steamer, they followed them beneath the water and saw that a huge chunk of wood was lodged between two of them. Tugging was to no avail and they surfaced to let the captain know. He tossed them a rope which they tied to the wood. Those on deck pulled when they felt the signal from beneath but nothing was gained. Whittingham ran in and joined them and soon Watson and Holmes were pulling also.

The men resurfaced. "It is not moving, Captain," one shouted. "The rope is not working. We must cut it out of there. Quick an axe, else soon we will be crocodile food!"

"Boy!" Ansari shouted to Whittingham. "To my quarters! On the wall to the left of the door are two axes. Fetch them as quickly as you can. The banks of the Nile are beginning to stir!"

Whittingham's terrified gaze darted to the far side of the river where tall reeds and muddy water thickened the shoreline. He saw the reeds sway, saw the ripple as the first crocodile slithered into the water. Before he could take another breath, he saw them. It seemed like hundreds, their tough ridged bodies breached the water, only their eyes visible, floating towards the steamer. He ran.

"Whittingham!" Sharrey stopped him in the hall. "What has happened?"

"Log jammed in the paddles! The men are going to try to cut it out of the way but the crocodiles are in the water! It is so dangerous, miss!, I really must go. They are depending on me!" Whittingham shouted over his shoulder. He took the stairs at a run, throwing open the door to the captain's quarters. Grasping the axes from the wall, he raced back. Terrified, excited, his heart pounding, he scanned the water.

"Look there, boy, they come from both sides of the river! You help watch and let the shooters know when those eyes go under water. That is their signal they will be striking. Stay alert!" the captain cried.

"You take the left, Whittingham, and I shall take the right. Spot for the shooters!" Watson called out and Whittingham ran to the rail, clutching with white knuckled fists.

"Captain if you have more weapons, Mr. Mitanni and I can help there," Holmes said.

"Of course, Mr. Holmes. Ari, give them your guns and fetch more. All help is welcome here."

The divers took the axes and disappeared into the water. They took turns cutting away at the wedged log and all the while the crocodiles skimmed the water moving in closer, effortlessly, noiselessly. Whittingham leaned over the rail, the sweat pouring from his brow and watched with eager eyes, eyes he dared not blink lest he miss a movement.

One of the divers surfaced and his eyes darted across the water. "It is half done, Captain," and he went under once more.

"There!" shouted Watson pointing. "There is one that is much too close!"

The men with the guns fired off several shots. The crocodile turned swiftly to another direction.

"There is one too close!" shouted Whittingham and his shooters fired, turning the beasts in another direction. Minutes passed and felt like hours. The sun beat down upon those on the deck yet they dared not move. The warning shots had steered off the approach of several crocodiles but they did not leave. They lingered, teasing the terror that gripped the men, gliding back and forth, becoming bolder with each turn in the water until one bulging set of eyes dared move forward once more.

"There!" Whittingham cried. "He went under just there!"

"Quick, Ari, get the men out of the water! The log will have to wait!" the captain shouted and more shots rang out, the hot lead hissing through the water. Ari put down his gun and reached for the first diver. Watson picked it up.

"No, no let me go and warn the others to come up!" the man cried.

Ari pulled up the first diver who scrambled up shaking and out of breath. They reached for the second man and Ari shouted, "Where is Mustaf?"

"He was almost through, he would not come!" cried one man.

"Mustaf?" the captain, shouted. "What a foolish man. His life is not worth a crocodile. There is nothing we can do. Boy! Watch the water! The crocodile will be gliding just beneath the surface now."

"He is there! I see him! I see him, Mr. Holmes, he is just there near the paddles!" Whittingham raced along the rail, following the shadow beneath the water.

Holmes aimed the gun at a sharp angle and quickly fired off several rounds, cursing for the delay in the reloading. Watson, who wanted to rush to help, knew he must stay vigilant where he was for the whole of the Nile appeared to have eyes. There was a thump against the boat. The crocodile flipped out of the water spinning over and over, his body turning, his tail thrashing, spewing blood into the water and the muddy Nile turned red.

"Quick! It is Mustaf! He is here!" cried one of the divers. They reached for the man, hoisting him to safety. His left arm was bleeding from several deep holes torn by the teeth of the crocodile, but he was alive.

"Dr. Watson! We need your help!" the captain shouted. "Quick, to my cabin! We will clean and dress it there. Mustaf you fool!"

"I may be the fool, Captain, but the crocodile got the better of that axe. I have lost it in his jaws, I am afraid, but I have dislodged the log from the paddles. It is safe to continue," Mustaf said with a toothless grin.

"We will set sail once you have been seen to," the captain said. "You old fool!"

It was several hours later that Watson had finally finished cleaning and stitching the torn flesh. Mustaf was helped to the men's quarters and given a strong sedative. Watson knew that once the shock of the attack wore off, the pain would set in and Mustaf would be miserable for quite some time.

"I must convey my thanks to you both, Mr. Holmes. You and Dr. Watson have been extremely helpful in saving Mustaf's life."

"We must add Whittingham to that also, Captain," Holmes said.

"Yes, where is the boy?"

"He has gone to help set things to right. It has been an exciting experience for him and I am sure we will hear of it for years to come," replied Holmes. "It is good your man is all right."

"Yes, and once again I thank you. Mustaf has been my ship's mate and good friend for many years. If there is anything you need, anywhere, anytime, Mr. Holmes," Ansari stretched out his hand, "you just say so. I am in your debt. Mustaf is in your debt. It is a life for a life out here and whatever we can do to repay you, we will."

"Thank you, Captain. It is much appreciated."

"But now that all the excitement is over, we shall stoke up the engines and see if those paddles work," the captain grinned.

Chapter Fourteen

A cool dawn enveloped the *Queen's Traveler* as she slowed her engines and off in the distance the sandstone buildings of Dashur slowly materialized. A lone villager spotted the ship slipping by and a high pitched shout rose from his throat, echoing across the water, stirring the inhabitants of the sleeping city. Soon there were hundreds of people milling about the streets, children running and laughing. Merchants were out setting up their shops, eager for the ship to turn about to unload their long awaited goods.

The steamer continued further south to a narrow jetty and the captain sent word to wake the passengers. Sharrey Princeton and Minnie Rothman dressed quickly and met the others on the deck just as the steamer's ropes were secured to the jetty. A ramp was set and soon Professor Princeton's party was safely on land. Princeton scanned the narrow path that wove across the desert. His workers would be arriving soon.

"We're here, Minnie!" Sharrey cried excitedly. "Look at this place! Look there! You can see the pyramids in the distance there. I can hardly wait!"

"But…but…there's nothing here but…desert!"

"That is the way of Egypt, Minnie," Mitanni said. "For miles upon miles there is nothing but desert."

"I don't know how you people ever get used to this sort of life. I am eager for this to be over and be on my way back to England!" Minnie exclaimed.

"Oh, Minnie! How can you say such things? We have only arrived and once we are able to visit with James, I am sure things will change," Sharrey said. "Oh dear! What is that coming?"

Moving towards them were hundreds of workers that seemed to appear out of nowhere, all excited and shouting at once. "Effendi! Effendi! You have been brought back safely! It is a blessing from the gods!"

"Yes, we have arrived safely. Thank you for coming so quickly, Maraq," Princeton said. "Now, gather the men and organize the work detail to unload the supplies and bring them back to the camp. And three of those donkeys are ours, also."

"Very good Effendi, it shall be done," the man bowed.

"Professor!" shouted Whittingham. "Did I hear you say three of those donkeys are coming with us?"

"Yes, we use them for transportation and many other things. Why?"

"There is one there, Professor, I am sure is a really hard worker. Do you think we could take that one?"

"It makes no never mind which one we take, boy, but as it appears important to you, I shall allow you to choose which three we take. They will be charged into your care. Be a good merchant now and choose wisely."

"Thank you!" Whittingham cried and raced back to the steamer. He ran to the donkey stall and threw his arms about Queenie's neck. "You will come with us, my girl, and I will make sure you are never treated badly. And we will take your friend the little black one there, and his friend, the gray one in the corner." Gripping the ropes, Whittingham led the three donkeys from the steamer.

The man called Maraq bowed, acknowledging Whittingham's choice of donkeys and began loading the luggage and supplies. Professor Princeton was with the captain, soon joined by Holmes and Watson.

"Thank you Captain, for a most memorable voyage," Watson said shaking his hand.

"It was memorable indeed, Dr. Watson. It was our good fortune to have had you and Mr. Holmes on board this trip. You saved the life of a very dear friend of mine."

"It was our pleasure," Watson said. "Safe journey back."

"Thank you," Ansari said. "Do not forget our debt, for once a debt such as this is incurred, it must be repaid."

"I will not forget, Captain," Holmes replied.

They began the long walk to the dig site. Minnie asked, "What is this effendi they call you, Professor?"

"It is their way of addressing anybody who is not of their own race. These men have been in my employ for years and are most trusted workers. We see to their care and we rarely have accidents. You will see, everyone looks out for everyone. It is a good crew. We must make haste before the sun begins to soar else we shall all perish. Come, it is a mile walk back to the dig site."

"That sounds a bit drastic," Minnie said.

"Not at all," Mitanni answered falling into step with the professor. "The workers begin their day before the sun has risen. Here in Egypt, the sun rises swiftly and becomes intolerably hot even more swiftly. Work stops for everyone by noon and does not resume until after four in the afternoon. Then the work does not end until sunset. It makes for a long day."

"You see the weather here is not anything like anywhere else in the world. Once the sun is at high noon, the temperature can soar to over 120 degrees. The dangers of sun and heat stroke compounded by dehydration are very real," Princeton added.

"Then why do you stay?" Minnie asked.

"Look around, Miss Rothman. Where else in the world could anyone ask for such peace and solitude, the beauty of ages and the wealth of knowledge of a civilization that is unsurpassed in architectural technology, astrology, religion and so much more."

"I agree, Father, I love it here," Sharrey put her arm through her father's. "I only wish you had allowed me to come sooner. I might have been a great help to you and James and your work."

Princeton pulled his arm free. "You do not know what you are saying and you should not have come. Your life is in danger, Sharrey, and you should not have come. That was the reason why you were left in England. To protect you, don't you see?"

"No, Father, I do not see!" Sharrey cried. The change in her father's demeanor angered her. "What I do see is you and James living and loving a land that is my heritage. My heritage! I am Egyptian, Father! You forget that my mother was a true Egyptian and I am her daughter. I would have loved to know her life, her beliefs, her loves! Not be sent away to be forgotten and unwanted!"

"I…I.." Princeton stuttered. "I did not know. I did not think you would…."

"That's right, Father! You don't know and you don't think! I have waited all my life for something, anything from you that would show me love. I was hoping that by coming here to help you and James that you might show something, anything, but I see you are incapable of that…"

"Miss Princeton," Holmes interrupted. "Perhaps this could be settled back at the dig site where there may be a bit more privacy. Then, Professor, you owe us all an explanation."

Holmes's piercing gray eyes stared at Princeton until the man looked away. "You are correct. We will discuss this back at the site. I should never have lost my temper, Sharrey, I am sorry. I will explain, I promise."

But the hurt and anger still burned inside Sharrey and she turned away from her father. She hung back and fell in step with Minnie behind the others. Minnie reached over, taking Sharrey's hand and gave it a squeeze. They slowed their pace and were quite some distance behind the others.

"Why does he do that, Minnie?" Sharrey finally cried.

"I don't know, Shar, but I'm sure he does not mean anything by it."

"Why doesn't he just tell me? Why doesn't he just explain? Can he not see how much I love him, how much I am growing to love Egypt? Oh, what's the use! I simply do not know how to reach him at all. Look, they are far up ahead talking as if nothing has happened. He makes me so angry!" she cried.

"I do not understand why you insist on shouting at the poor girl," Watson was saying to the professor. "She has done nothing but have your best interests at heart."

"As do I with hers, Dr. Watson. I know I have come across as an unloving and uncaring parent, but that is far from the truth. I am very grateful to both you and Mr.

Holmes for escorting Sharrey safely here, but here is not where she should be."

"And you have yet to tell us why," Holmes said.

"It involves the ring and the box that I sent to her, Mr. Holmes."

"We had deduced that much, Professor. But why? Why would you send such a thing to her and not explain anything to her or to anyone," Holmes said.

"I will tell you this much. The ring and the box belonged to my wife, Sari Nefrati. She had the items in her family for generations. They date back to the Pharaoh Snefru, you know. She told me about them, but it wasn't until she found herself pregnant with Sharrey, that she explained to me what they really meant. I really wanted Berihun to tell the story because he is a direct descendant of the magi, the secret ancient bodyguards of the pharaoh."

"You must be joking!" Watson exclaimed.

"Not at all my good doctor. Berihun and Bashan, he was my servant who was struck down by the viper in the canobic jar, I am sure Sharrey mentioned that to you. Well, they and many others are direct descendants of the magi, and have guarded the pharaohs and their descendants for generations....well to be exact even to now. Bashan was with Sari and I. He was assigned to Sari from the day she was born for it was on her birth that her mother gave to her the possession of the ring and the box and it was to Bashan it fell to protect them both.

"When Sari knew she was pregnant and she knew it was a girl, don't ask me how, but the woman just knew things, she told me of the significance of them. She said that whoever was in possession of them would have control over the peoples of Egypt and its riches. The only reason she told me this was because she feared she would not live to tell Sharrey herself. And in that, she was correct. She was very ill following the birth, and lived long enough to hold her in her arms one time and to name her. That was the most tragic day of my life and it should have been one of the happiest."

"But what does her death have to do with the ring and the box?" Holmes asked.

"Don't you see? Don't you see what that ring and box would hold for Sharrey? Don't you see the danger she could be in if anyone discovered the true meaning of them?"

"But surely that is a legend, a pharaoh's tale, a …a…" Watson stumbled for the right word.

"A curse? That is exactly what it is. A curse! I sent her away to England to be safe. I kept the ring and the box here with me to protect her."

"So what changed? What happened that you felt desperate enough to send those items to her knowing the danger she would be in?" Holmes asked.

"The British. It all began when the British seized control of Africa. Suddenly there were countries and nations of people who demanded to be in control of Egypt. The British, the Turks, the French and heaven only knows how many others are out there. All of these nations are in control of their own country yet cannot see that Egyptians should be in control of Egypt. But it's all about greed, you see. Egypt is a very rich country. It has jewels, gold and so many other riches that are the envy of everyone around us. There is a great struggle within for control of Egypt and it has yet to surface. But surface it will and it will mean death for many."

"When that incident happened with the snake killing Bashan, I knew it was not an accident. Even I know that a snake could not live in a sealed jar from thousands of years ago, but to the locals, of course, it became part of the pharaoh's curse. I do not understand what happened to James, but I know that was no accident either, nor was it a curse. It was a matter of time before whose ever hand was in the pot for control would find the ring and the box and all hope for Egypt would be lost. Bashan had stayed with me because it was his duty to protect them and it cost him his life. I summoned his magi brother, Berihun and sent him to England with the items to protect them and Sharrey. I felt they would be safer out of the country. But here, you have brought them both back. Back into the lair of the evil that lurks about to take control of this mighty civilization. It is a tragedy waiting to happen."

"And you have no idea who may be involved?" Holmes asked.

"Not a clue. I am an archeologist, Mr. Holmes, not a detective. I have tried to protect my daughter and my country from danger and destruction and I am afraid I am failing miserably at both."

"I am a detective and Watson and I will stay and find out who is involved in this. But you, you underestimate yourself, Professor, for we are still in possession of the ring and the box and Sharrey is still alive. She is very hurt and angry with you and once we are settled in at the dig site, you should summon your daughter and explain all of this to her," Holmes said.

"You are correct, of course. And I must apologize for my behavior earlier. I am truly grateful that you have brought her safely thus far and would wish for you to continue. I believe we are in need of your services after all."

"Look, up ahead. I see your compound of tents, Professor. I did not realize how enormous such an undertaking an excavation would be."

"That happens to most people, Dr. Watson. They forget that not only do we have to have tents to house everyone including the workers, but we need accommodations for food and water, for supplies and for storing the artifacts that we find. It is a huge undertaking and greatly misunderstood by many," Princeton said.

"I see," Watson said. "At last we have arrived."

Chapter Fifteen

He stood waiting at the entrance of the tent, watching for signs of the party. Everyone had heard the cries of the workers approaching and they quickly made preparations. "I see them, Master James. They are coming now."

James rose from the chair anxiously. "Who is there?"

"There are two men with your father, immersed in deep conversation. Behind is another I do not know and far behind them, are the two women. What shall we do?"

"Let me think," James sat on the edge of the bed twisting the ends of the sheets. "Here's what we will do. I want you to meet them. Tell them that I have improved a little, just a little, Chibale. Tell them that I have been able to sit up but that I am in a daze and have not spoken yet. Tell them it is a good sign of the gods for their safe return."

"That is a good plan. I will do as you wish. Now lie down and I will go." Chibale waited for James to reposition himself on the bed then set out of the tent. As he neared the group of people approaching, he quickened his step.

"Professor! Professor Princeton!" He shouted. "The gods above have blessed your return with good news!"

"What is it, Chibale!" Princton exclaimed. "Is it James? Has something happened?"

"Yes, Professor, it is good news," Chibale caught up to them and bowed deeply. "I was speaking to him early this morning, as is my custom, regarding your return and he made a movement, Professor. He moved his arm and his fingers, Professor. And just now, when I called to him that you were approaching, he moved again!"

"Sharrey! It is James!" Princeton shouted to the two women some distance away.

"What did he say, Minnie? I cannot hear over the constant chanting of these workers."

"It sounds like he said something has happened to James." They looked at each other in alarm, then pulled up their skirts and ran.

"It is James, Sharrey. Chibale here said James tried to move. He is excited about our return and has tried to move!" Princeton exclaimed drawing Sharrey to him in a warm embrace.

"If he has tried to move, then he must be able to understand," Watson said. "Perhaps it might prove beneficial if I examined him, Professor. Perhaps another medical opinion may be warranted."

"We shall see, Dr. Watson. Oh Sharrey, it is most exciting news!" They hurried ahead. Behind them Chibale followed with Minnie and Colter. Holmes put a hand to Watson's arm, drawing him back.

"What! What is it, Holmes? The change in James's condition is good news don't you agree?"

"Yes, I do Watson. I also find it a bit convenient that his condition should improve suddenly upon our return and that the news should be brought to us by Chibale?" Holmes queried.

Watson's brows went up. "Chibale! Why that is the…"

"Yes it is. The connection with Miss Rothman and the message on the ship."

"Holmes! You do not think that James Princeton and Minnie Rothman are in this together, do you? Harm Sharrey? His own sister, simply for possession of that ring and the box?"

"If what is being told to us is correct, that ring and box hold the wealth and power of Egypt. All one has to do is possess them. With that strong a motive, anything is possible, Watson."

"But that is all superstition! How can a ring and a box hold the power and wealth over a nation?" cried Watson.

"It wouldn't be the ring and the box, Watson. It would be the beliefs behind them that would give the bearer power. Don't you see how superstitious these people are? They still believe in their old gods and customs. If and when the news of the arrival of the ring and the box surfaces, there will be an uprising among the people here and a pressure to believe and follow those old customs along with the one who possesses ownership. That is a mighty strong incentive to gain possession of them, don't you agree? Let us meet this James Princeton."

They walked into the tent, Chibale nodded to them as they entered. "Oh James," Sharrey was kneeling beside the bed where he was lying. "James, it is Sharrey. I've come all this way to see you and be with you. I was going to bring you home to England, James, but I have decided to stay. I shall stay and take care of you and Father and learn of my homeland. And you shall help me, James. I am very excited. And I've brought a surprise with me, James. Look! Look, here is Minnie. You remember Minnie?" Sharrey motioned for Minnie to come forward.

"Oh, James, it's Minnie. It's me, James." She bent to kiss his cheek.

"My dear, James has only just begun to improve," Princeton said. "We must not expect too much too soon, must we."

"No, Father, but it is so good to see him. He looks so healthy and alive. It is hard to believe he has been in such a state for weeks," Sharrey said. "But it does not matter. Not any more James for Minnie and I are here to take care of you and bring you back to us. Right, Minnie?"

"Yes, you and I will see to it that James wants for nothing and we will nurse him back," Minnie smiled at Sharrey.

"Professor," Watson said. "I can examine James if you wish. Perhaps there is something I can do for him."

"That is not necessary," Chibale stepped between Watson and the Professor. "We have had many physicians here and we are doing all that needs to be done."

"Chibale is correct, Dr. Watson. There is no need for you to reexamine James. All that can be done is being done. But thank you for offering. Maraq, please show them to their quarters."

"As you wish, Effendi," Maraq bowed. "Please to come this way?"

The tent they were led to was some distance away Two cots, one on either side with a small table and lamp in the center, with a wash stand, a pitcher of water and a small towel. Watson eased onto a cot and sighed.

"I have your bags, sirs," Whittingham popped his head inside. "This is fantastic, don't you think, Dr. Watson?" he deposited Watson's bag and valise. "Your bags, Mr. Holmes," he added returning with Holmes's bags.

"Thank you, Whittingham, that will be all for now. You had best see to the stabling of those little beasts of yours since Professor Princeton has made you the keeper of the herd," Holmes said.

"I will gratefully tend to them, Mr. Holmes, but I will not shirk my duties to you and Dr. Watson either. If there is anything else you would like, I will return in an hour, sir."

"No, young man, there is nothing else we require this afternoon. Take care of those donkeys and find a shady place to crawl into. The sun is getting hotter by the second. Give them and yourself plenty of water."

"I will, sir, no fear of that. I will see you this evening." Whittingham ran back to the animals.

Holmes watched the boy for several moments before returning to his cot, his elbows to his knees, clenched fists to his chin. "Watson, there is something amiss with James. Miss Princeton said it all in her statement that he looked so healthy after such a lengthy stay in a catatonic state. He has been faking the entire episode, I am sure, and Chibale is part of it. Why else would he step in declining your examination? Chibale is a servant and spoke out of turn. It was not his decision to make."

"That is true, Holmes. I watched James and his reactions to the ladies. His eyes had rapid movement, his hand moved as well and there was a marked increase in his breathing. Someone in a true catatonic state would not have those reactions. Obviously he was well aware of what was happening around him."

"Yes, I noticed, also, grateful that your medical expertise has verified that. The question is should we expose him for the fraud that he is or not."

"Just what I was pondering myself, but what good would come of it, Holmes? If we expose him now, we would still not know if it is James for sure who is after the ring and the box. I still have my doubts that he would partner up with Miss Rothman to endanger his sister just for the sake of the thing."

"That's it!" Holmes exclaimed. "That's it!" He crossed to the entrance, peering out in all directions. He pulled the flap over the opening, turned to Watson and continued in a low whisper, "You have hit it right on the head, Watson! Perhaps James and Miss Rothman aren't alone. Perhaps there is someone else."

"You mean with James and Miss Rothman or in addition to?"

"Think back on the history both Miss Princeton and her father told us about. What if James questioned him about the reasons why she was kept in England and why suddenly he was now sending a bodyguard along with the items to her there. Princeton would naturally feel obligated to explain, James being his son and all.

"Now Miss Princeton mentioned that her brother had become friendly with Miss Rothman during the infrequent visits to England over the years. Let's say he sent Miss Rothman a letter instructing her to make sure Sharrey comes to Egypt and to be sure to bring back the ring and the box."

"Yes, and Miss Princeton said that Miss Rothman was the one who insisted she come to Egypt for her father and her brother's safety. She also agreed to accompany her, a fact which was her idea in the first place, to be sure. But how would that account for all those attempts on Miss Princeton's life? If they are only after the ring and the box, Miss Princeton would simply give it to her brother if he asked, for she so much as said she hated the thing," Watson said.

"Yes she would, which is why there is another party involved. There is someone else who is after that ring and box, someone who is willing to kill to get it. Fool! Fool that I've been not seeing it sooner. A second adversary explains the unanswered questions, ties all the loose ends, Watson!" Holmes exclaimed.

"Unanswered questions? Loose ends?" Watson cried.

"Yes, it explains why Miss Rothman was genuinely shocked at the attempt on Miss Princeton's life, shocked at the attack on Whittingham. She and James had no intention of hurting anyone. They knew Miss Princeton would simply hand the items over to them if asked. All they needed to do was get her to Egypt. That is why we are now going to see a marked improvement in James."

"Holmes!" Watson shouted when Holmes turned and rushed out. "Where are you off to? The temperature is searing out there! You will not last long in the sun!"

"I do not intend to go very far. I simply need to think. I cannot do that in the confines of that tent!" Holmes called over his shoulder.

"Come, my dear. I will take you and Miss Rothman to your tent," Peter Princeton said "When you wired you were coming, I had Maraq's people see to your accommodations. I know how important a woman's privacy is. They have done well, you will like it I am sure."

Sharrey tucked her arm into her father's. "I cannot believe how hot it has gotten in just the few minutes we have been with James. Why it was just moments ago that we arrived and it was not this hot!" she exclaimed.

"It is Egypt, my dear. I will have a servant bring fresh water and something light to eat. Mind you, it will be warm, but it will be clean. You ladies can freshen up, then have a quiet lie down out of this heat. The day will start in earnest once more after four, then I will show you the pyramid of Snefru, where my dig site is located."

"Oh, I am so excited to be here!" she exclaimed. "Don't start again, Father. I came here to bring you and James back to England to be rid of this curse that is affecting everyone and everything. But I have changed my mind. I have decided to stay. No! Do not look at me like that. I am a grown woman, capable of making my own decisions and I have decided to stay, Father. Colter has…"

"Colter? What has Colter to do with this?" Princeton exclaimed.

"Colter has been teaching me of the Egyptian culture. He has promised that when James is well we will all go to learn of the sites at Saqqara, and at Giza and here at Dashur and he told me he will take me to the Valley of the Kings and to Karnak, even though it holds tragic memories for him for that is where his parents were killed. Did you know that, Father?" Sharrey quickly changed the subject.

"Yes, I had heard of the accident but by then Colter was nearly a grown man. I tried to get in touch with him but he seemed to just disappear for a few months and I lost tract after that. Ah, here we are," he said stopping in front of a very large tent.

He pushed aside the heavy rug that covered the entrance and they stepped inside to a very dark and very cool space. A small lamp on the center table showed them several spaces divided by woven hangings. Each area held a cot, a small table with a lamp, a basin and pitcher of water and a cloth. There was a set of low tables at the end of each cot and their heavy trunks had already been placed there. Their smaller bags were on the cots.

"Oh, Father!" Sharrey exclaimed. "I have never seen anything so beautiful!"

"Some of the workmen live in Dashur and when I told them I needed something special for my daughter, news spread throughout the city of the great English ladies that were coming. They insisted on making these preparations. I am pleased you like it."

"It is beautiful!" Minnie exclaimed. "It is as if they decorated for a queen."

"That they did, Miss Rothman," Princeton said looking lovingly at his daughter. "That they did."

Princeton left the women, returning to James's tent. "Ah, Colter," he said to Mitanni upon entering, "I see you already have your things inside."

"Yes, thank you Professor. I see Sharrey's presence is good for James. He is sitting in a chair and every so often, I can see him make an attempt to move his hand. Chibale is very good at taking care of his needs."

"Yes he is, Colter. I'm hoping Mr. Holmes will be able to put an end to this 'curse' that has hounded us these several weeks. Perhaps it is a sign of the gods that Sharrey has come to Egypt."

"It is her rightful heritage, Professor. She needs to know about her mother, whether you wish to speak of her or not."

"I know, but it is such a delicate subject. But…when the right time comes, I will tell her. For now, it is good she is here, for James's sake. I am not so sure of her own. Berihun is at her tent. He will guard her well. Now I must get out of this heat. But first I must see to the inventory of goods and the animals."

"No need, sir. That young lad, Whittingham has taken care of the animals. And I must admit has seen to the accounting and storage of the supplies with Maraq. He has a sound head for mathematics as well as organization. Maraq is enjoying having an apprentice so willing to learn. And the animals follow him everywhere. I must say he is very good with them."

"Perhaps I shall hire him on," Princeton laughed.

"It is no laughing matter, Professor. That boy loves them. He would consider it an honor not only to take care of them but to work for you and be able to stay in Egypt."

"I will give that some thought. I will see you later."

Chapter Sixteen

"**O**h Minnie, this is so exciting, isn't it?" Sharrey cried.

"I dare say it is, Shar. Look at this! Who would believe something so elegant would exist out here. I prefer this left side, if you don't mind," Minnie said.

"Not at all. You should choose after all, you are the guest. I am staying so that makes me your hostess. Oh, Minnie!" Sharrey fell back on the cot. Her eyes caught the hand stitched tapestries that were placed as room dividers and she followed the design down them. There were hieroglyphics and pictographs of the gods and goddesses and the pharaohs and their queens woven into it. They told a story of a mighty nation, of the births of the sons and the daughters, the deaths of the ancient ones and their elaborate burial rituals and chambers. They told of the riches of the flowing waters of the Nile and those along her shores and buried deep beneath her caverns. Gold bracelets and arm bands, rich opulent jewels of diamonds, emeralds and rubies were made to stand out using ancient techniques of weaving and dyeing.

But there were also the riches that belonged to the poor. The Nile flooding her banks each year depositing rich soil for the growing of cotton, of wheat and flax; trees of figs and dates; men, women and children working the fields, netting fish from the water, making bricks, moving massive stones for the building of the pyramids.

The riches of Egypt, Sharrey thought. They are not just the gold and diamonds are they, Mother. It is the land. It is the people. They make up all the riches for without them there would be no Egypt. She spoke to the spirit of the mother she had never known, yet somehow here in this land of ancient rituals, beliefs and knowledge, she had a feeling that her mother was there beside her, filling her with the knowledge and wisdom she would someday come to need.

"You know, Minnie," Sharrey began but when she glanced over, Minnie Rothman had fallen to sleep. "I probably should too if I want to be up to exploring Father's excavations," she mumbled to herself. She reached to move her bag and saw there was a note beneath it. Opening it she read, 'If you wish to know the secret of the ring and the box meet me at the stone wall near the dig site.'

Chapter Seventeen

Watson was lying down fanning himself with the pages of an old newspaper when Holmes returned.

"I've taken a turn about the camp and there is nothing that appears untoward," he said.

"That is a good sign, is it not?" Watson looked over to him. "Sit man, you look terribly done in. Have some water. It does no good to run oneself out when strength and energy may be needed soon."

"Of course." Holmes took a swallow and spit it out. "But this is as warm as the wind outside! It has risen quite suddenly and is blowing that wretched sand about. If it worsens the professor will have to cancel work for the day. But worse, it will also restrict any investigating I might wish to do. Damn it all!"

"Lie down, Holmes. It is several hours yet before the workers will be up and about. No sense fretting over anything yet. So, there is nothing interesting going on out there?"

"You misunderstand my words, Watson. It *appears* there is nothing untoward, but I did have Maraq show me the storage tent."

"And?" Watson prompted, resuming his fanning.

"It isn't really a tent, old man. It is a small building of stone and mortar that has been hastily put together to store the trinkets that are found. Shelves line all the walls and they are fairly full of ancient artifacts. Maraq remained at the entrance too afraid to enter, and pointed out the canobic jar and the container that Professor Princeton sealed the said papers in. I had a chance to look around but of course things have been greatly disturbed since then. However!"

"However?"

"On investigation, I discovered that the seal on the canobic jar had been tampered with but the work was so well camouflaged that it had to have been done by an expert. Right down to putting the ageing touches around the lid. There was a tiny hole on the underside of the lid, an air hole for the snake no doubt, else the snake would not have survived for long. Very ingenious indeed, but had the Professor or even James really studied the thing, I am sure they would have discovered this for themselves. I then took the container and removed the pages that James was purported to be reading that fateful day and made my discovery. Naturally I was not able to decipher the hieroglyphics that were written there but I certainly could detect the faint but lingering odor of poison. And you know me, Watson, I know my poisons."

"So what was it?" Watson swung his legs over the side of the bed to listen more intently, for Holmes once more had lowered his voice.

"It was a combination of several very poisonous substances, in point of fact. A droplet had fallen to the parchment and once dried there became a dried spot appearing as a smudge. There was a sufficient amount to determine the types of drugs used. The first I could detect was datura stramonium. As you know this intoxicating drug comes from the jimson weed and possesses strong hallucinogenic qualities. Even the minutest vapor inhaled would make a person lightheaded."

"That would account for the professor thinking the writing on the parchment actually moved," Watson said.

"Exactly!" Holmes exclaimed. "There must have been enough of that drug still present to cause that hallucinatory sensation in him. There was also a very deadly drug that is extracted from a toad called bufo marinus or the cane toad. Not only is the fluid that is extracted poisonous, but the toad itself is deadly to any predator that consumes it. Again a third poison called tetrodoxin, which is a deadly poison extracted from the puffer fish. When ingested it stops the heart from beating, causing suffocation and death. In each of these drugs lies enough danger to cause death, but combined together with exactly the right quantities can produce the catatonic state that we see in James. Does this remind you of anything, Watson?"

"You don't mean voodoo such as we discovered on our Brakenberry case?" Watson cried.

"One and the same. Over in West Africa, the voodoo cult is practiced as a religion but is known as Vodun. The Mama or Queen Mother rules the tribe and has the wisdom of the ages of the tribal medicines and would know exactly how to obtain and mix the three poisons to produce what we call the zombie, a person alive but not alive. It is this mixture of drugs that produces such a condition, Watson."

"But who? Why?"

"I don't know that just yet. But we are dealing with a very deadly combination of poisons and someone who means to stop at nothing until they have control of the ring and the box. The one fact that most people do not know, however, is that such effects do wear off after several days if the person is not subjected to another dose.

The mixture must have been placed over James's nose and mouth just long enough to render him unconscious but not enough to actually kill him. Apparently whoever had done this wanted him alive."

"For what reason?"

"It is clear that James's death would have caused a stir here and there would be inquiries, to be sure. With him simply in a catatonic state and unconscious, it would be attributed to the curse of the pharaohs, and that alone would be enough to bring Miss Princeton running to Egypt with the ring and the box. And that is exactly what has happened. It seems we all walked right into the trap that was set, Watson."

"But how were we to know, Holmes. We were engaged by Miss Princeton only to see her safe arrival in Egypt and bring her brother and father back home to England with her. Had we known the full story regarding the ring and the box, perhaps our course of action may have been different."

"I'm sure it would have, old man. But as it is, we have brought her and the ring and the box right into the midst of the lion's den. This upheaval in rulership that Professor Princeton speaks of is coming, that is obvious. Another obvious fact is that whoever poisoned James did so with his full knowledge and consent else why would he have played the part for so long? I do not like this, Watson, I do not like this at all. This links James to Minerva Rothman and James to whomever else is involved."

"It also links...well, everyone with everyone when you get right down to it, Holmes."

"Yes, it most certainly does."

Chapter Eighteen

Sharrey debated for more than an hour before deciding not to wake Minnie and tell her of the note. But when she pushed aside the cover over the door, Berihun was standing there. "Oh, Berihun! In this heat? Step inside and have some water. It is warm but it is water."

"Thank you, but," Berihun bowed entering. He turned, "you are not coming in?"

"No, actually, I have to…well…I must…How do men say…A call of nature? I do hope you have no intention to follow me there, Berihun?" she inquired with raised brows. "Surely I will be safe there!"

"No mistress, but I…"

"Good. Go get that drink and I will be right back." Sharrey let the cover fall into place and looked about. Off in the distance the top of the pyramid was barely visible through the haze that now enveloped the dig site. All work had stopped and the entire place was silent except for the howling of the wind. A pallid sun shone smoky and vaporous in the sky, an ominous sign in the quiet bleakness of the site. She saw the trail that led towards the pyramid dig site and in mere seconds made up her mind. Berihun was already shifting the cover. She had to get away!

She pulled her handkerchief from her sleeve and put it to her face to ward off the biting sand, then stepped into the wind. It was some distance to the site and there were many twists and turns. Moving cautiously to avoid blowing debris, she soon neared the bend in the path which narrowed itself between two rising pillars of stone that gave a brief respite from the stinging sand.

Here she stopped to get her bearings. Up ahead the sand swirled with reckless abandon and for several long moments she stared in front of her, uncertain whether she should continue or turn back. The storm was far more wicked than she had anticipated and her resolve to continue began to falter. A lull in the wind, a scant moment of clarity and she saw the shadowy outline of the pyramid looming ahead. Her resolve returned and she continued. Several more feet and she came to the stone wall that was mentioned in the note, an extension of the ancient palisade that once surrounded the pyramid of the Pharaoh Snefru.

The wall, once a twenty foot tall structure built to enclose the pyramid complex, had been abandoned and neglected for thousands of years. Many of the stones had been taken and reused to build other structures and there were only remnants left behind. Sharrey leaned against the stones, clinging to them for support, using them for protection against the storm as she continued along the path.

Over the din of the storm she heard shouting, faint and indistinct and she cocked her head to listen. She turned to see Berihun nearly upon her. He had followed her! He had found her out! Panic gripped her at the sight of him running at her, his arms waving wildly, shouting something she could not nor did she want to hear. Her mind thought of the note! She needed to find out what the ring and the box meant! Her heart pounded; with a last look at Berihun, she turned in a panic to get away, to escape. But she was already too late. The wall above her began to collapse.

Berihun lunged forward, shoving Sharrey to the ground, her screams lost in the storm. The stone wall came down, tumbling and smashing, showering them with stones. Sharrey lay beneath Berihun, her hands clutched into fists over her face. Berihun had landed on his hands and knees above her, the weight of the stone upon his back.

"Hurry, my Queen! You must pull yourself out!" He cried.

"I…I can't!"

"You must. Do you not see? I cannot hold this much longer. It is the weight of the wall and it is coming down upon us. You must escape for it is your life that is the more worthy."

His face mere inches away, Sharrey felt the splats of blood that dripped from Berihun's face. His cheek was torn open, an ugly jagged cut where he was wedged against a large stone. His arms, spread on either side of her were beginning to quiver and she saw the muscles tense as the weight of the rock grew increasingly more than he could bear.

"Oh Berihun, you have saved my life this second time, how can you say mine is more worthy? You are…"

"Get out!" He shouted at her. "You must get out do you hear? You are the rightful queen of Egypt and must be protected. Get out!" His face reddened, he dared hardly breathe, the veins bulged at the sides of his neck and Sharrey could count every beat of his heart with each pulse that raced through those veins.

Shaken and afraid, Sharrey scrambled out from beneath Berihun and he could hold out no longer. His arms and legs gave way and he collapsed beneath the rubble of stone.

"*No!*" Sharrey screamed. She pulled at the stones, hurling them aside, groping through the rubble where she'd last seen his face. Dark trickles of blood spread into the sand, and at last she was able to uncover his face. "Hold on Berihun, I will get help. Hold on!"

Sharrey scrambled to her feet. She gripped the folds of her dress and ran back stumbling blindly along the path. She ran headlong into Colter Mitanni and was vaguely aware of his arms around her.

"Oh, Colter! Help! You must help! It's Berihun!" she cried, gasping for breath.

"Sharrey! What happened? You are hurt, you are bleeding! Let me get you back…"

"No…no you must help Berihun. He saved my life! He…the wall…the stone wall…it fell and he saved my life. Oh Colter! He is trapped beneath the stones!" She burst into wracking sobs, finally realizing the full extent of what had happened.

"Where?" Colter shook her. "Tell me where?"

"The stone wall! It was my fault…Colter!" she cried.

"Listen! Listen to me!" He pulled her to her feet. "I will go help Berihun. You run back and get more help. I cannot do this alone. Do you hear me? Do you understand?"

Sharrey sobbed and nodded. "I do…I will…go Colter! Save him!" She pushed him aside and once more reached for her skirts, running and shouting for help.

Colter struggled against the wind, fighting every step to get to the stone wall. Stumbling into the recent fall, he saw Berihun's head and reached down to check for signs of life. Yes! There was but only just. He was madly tossing stones, breathless when the others arrived.

"Hurry, move those stones,! Someone..." shouted Professor Princeton. "Someone go protect his head!"

"I will do that," Watson hurried to him, cradling Berihun's head in the protection of his arms. "He is still alive, barely breathing, but still alive. You must hurry!"

"Sharrey get out of here!" Princeton shouted to his daughter. "Let the men take care of this!"

"I cannot, Father! This is the second time he has saved my life! No! Do not stop me!" Sharrey screamed at him and backed away.

Peter Princeton saw the blazing determination in her eyes and for one fleeting moment he saw Sari Nefrati. Yes, he thought immediately, this will be the woman to help save Egypt. He nodded and together they began to remove the stones.

The blowing sand was relentless, blinding their vision, choking in throats and noses, gagging them. It filled in the cavities left by a removed stone before they could remove the next. Hands reached in to scoop the sand, reached in to remove stones, hands worked furiously in the storm until finally Berihun was uncovered. The workmen gathered around to protect him.

"A stretcher! Carefully. Do not twist him if possible. Keep him as straight as possible. Do not move his head. I have not had time to fully examine him!" Watson shouted at the workmen.

"Let them work, Dr. Watson. They have done this many times. They will get him to the tent safely," Princeton said. He fell into step with Watson and Berihun was taken into the infirmary.

"Now everyone out!" Watson shouted. "I will need water. Plenty of water. And bandages. Plenty of bandages. And clean washcloths. Plenty of washcloths. Now go!"

Everyone hurried to gather the supplies Watson needed while Holmes pulled a chair near the door. He watched Watson expertly take command of his work, lending a hand to help when needed, then just as quickly, stepping out of the way.

Watson cleaned the wounds and saw that most of Berihun's injuries were fairly superficial. A few knots on the head and a concussion, several cuts, bleeding but not serious. The deep cut along his cheekbone, however, would require several stitches. He washed and stitched, then wrapped his head in clean bandaging. He then carefully felt along the arms and legs for any broken bones or factures and to his amazement found none. He did notice a soft mushy tone to the upper portion of Berihun's arms. The falling stone had done some damage to the muscle tissue possibly tearing the tendons and ligaments. But they would heal.

He then felt the stomach and back, noticing severe bruising behind the shoulder blades. A groan came from the big man when Watson applied pressure to the area beneath the blades. "I see here is the problem, Holmes. Both sides I am afraid. The man has several broken ribs. I will have to wait until he awakes for I need him to sit upright so I can wrap those ribs tightly and properly in order to heal right."

"The man took a beating out there, Watson," Holmes said.

"He did just that. I can't believe he held those stones as he did. That is a man determined in his quest, that's for sure."

Berihun's eyes opened and rolled. "Where is Miss Princeton," he muttered from swollen lips.

"She is safe and well. I will see to her after I have taken care of you. Now I need you to sit up so I can wrap those broken ribs."

"I must get back…"

"You must do nothing of the sort," Watson eased him up. "You are lucky to be alive, Berihun, and there will be many weeks of rest before you will get back to work. You have a concussion, several cuts and bruises on your head, your eye is swelled, your muscles have been severely injured and will needs weeks to heal and you have several broken ribs that I can count. Now, man, I will help you to sit up, you will allow me to wrap those ribs, then you will rest for several weeks. Holmes and I will see to the care of Miss Princeton until you are able."

Watson rolled the cotton gauze about Berihun's chest, then helped him to lie back down. "Now Holmes, if you would be so kind, stay with this man while I tend to Miss Princeton," he said.

Berihun gripped Watson's arm tightly. "You must bring her here. You must bring them all here, Dr. Watson. I have to tell all of you, please. I must do it now."

"Very well. I will see to Miss Princeton's injuries and will bring her here, and you should rest until I return."

"I will rest when all is said."

Chapter Nineteen

With Berihun safely in the infirmary, Colter escorted Sharrey back to her tent. Minnie rose with a start when they entered.

"What happened!" Minnie gathered the water basin and towel while Colter helped Sharrey to the cot. "Oh Shar, I don't know where to begin!" she cried. "You are covered in dirt and blood!"

"Here give me that. At least I know where I hurt the most." Sharrey took the towel and began to dab at her face. "I cannot believe what just happened!"

"Just what did happen!" demanded Colter. "With everything that has been going on, what on earth possessed you to go out there alone? You could have been seriously hurt! Have you any idea how dangerous it is out there?"

Sharrey began to cry. "Stop it Colter! Can't you see she is hurt enough!" Minnie shouted at him.

"And it is her own fault! She has brought this upon herself and she has caused her bodyguard to be seriously injured if not dead. Did you not think before you went out there?"

"*No!*" Sharrey sobbed. "I did not think and for that I am sorry. But there was a note. A note telling me to come to the pyramid if I wanted to know the truth...I...don't you see how sorry I am! I know what I have done, what I have caused. I do not care to my injuries. But Berihun! All he ever tried to do was protect me and I have caused him such grievous injury. He...he...he just ran in front of me...he...he...pushed me down and threw himself on top of me to protect me from the stones! I was in such shock... I could not believe what was happening. I should never have gone, but I did and it is done. It is Berihun who is suffering because of me, but it is I who must live with this thing that I have done. Can't you leave me alone! Just go! Leave me alone! Both of you!" Sharrey cried. "Just go!"

Minnie started to protest, but she too, was angry. What had Sharrey done? How did Berihun get injured protecting her? Protecting her from what? There were so many unanswered questions and a mounting number of violent and cruel attacks on the members of their party. None of this had been part of the plan! With a hateful look at Colter, she stormed out. Colter followed behind her and she turned on him.

"Are you happy? What happened? What on earth happened out there?" Minnie cried.

"We don't really know, Minnie. And yes I am sorry. I lost my temper and I should not have. It is just that I am so concerned for her. I love her you know," Colter said point blank.

"I know, Colter, we all know. It is so obvious your feelings for her. It hangs out on your sleeve like some lovesick puppy and...well, we just all know. I didn't mean to shout at you either. I, too, am concerned. I was napping and when I woke, she was gone. I don't know what was going on. Oh for goodness sake, now what!"

Watson called out. "Miss Princeton! Is she all right?"

"Thank goodness you have come, Dr. Watson. She is inside there and I am afraid we were terribly cross with her for acting so foolish," Minnie said. "I hope she is more tolerant of you. Please see to her. She looks terrible."

Watson nodded, calling out as he entered, "Miss Princeton, it is me, Dr. Watson. May I enter?"

He barely heard the weak yes and he went in to find her lying on the cot. He took in her bloodstained clothes, her hands and face scraped and bruised. "My dear, you look dreadful!"

"Thank you, Dr. Watson. I believe those are the words most women long to hear," she smiled weakly up at him and struggled to sit up.

"No, no do not move. I must examine you I am afraid, and lying down is the best position for that. I apologize for the insult. It was not meant as one. I was simply stating a fact. Here, allow me to examine for any broken or fractured bones first. I am afraid this is an intrusive procedure but it must be done."

"I understand, Dr. Watson."

A few minutes of silence while Watson conducted his examination. Finding nothing broken, he heaved a sigh of relief. "There, that is done. I apologize my dear. But the good news is that everything is very much intact. Not so good for Berihun, I'm afraid. Broken ribs and a concussion, but he will mend."

"Oh, Dr. Watson!" Sharrey burst into tears once more. "I am so sorry for causing his injuries!"

"My dear Miss Princeton! What has happened is not your fault. Berihun was doing his duty in protecting you. He knew and still knows the consequences of his duties and is prepared to fulfill them. Rest assured he holds no blame to you. None at all. Now if you are able, you must sit up for me. Let's see if we can't wash some of that desert from your face and hands, shall we?"

"You are such a blessing. Both you and Mr. Holmes. I don't know what I would have done if your tent had not been so close for me to go for help. And you, rushing to gather everyone else. Thank you... Ouch!"

"So sorry. You do have a nasty cut on your forehead that requires a bandage. Many scrapes and scratches that will heal with no scarring. Your hands are very bruised and bleeding, but will also heal. They will hurt for some time, but will get better. There, now that the bandage is in place I will give you the opportunity to change into something fresh. Berihun has requested you and your father. There is something he wishes to say. Please, do not refuse. It is extremely important to him."

"Oh, how can I face him, Dr. Watson? After what I have done? How can I ever face anyone ever again?" Sharrey burst into a fresh wash of tears.

Watson rinsed the washcloth and lifting her chin with one finger, began to clean the tears from her face once more. "Now let me explain something to you, my dear. Berihun was assigned as your bodyguard. He will do whatever it takes to protect you from harm. He knows that. He knows the consequences and knowing all of that, he has grown very fond of you and is willing to give his life for you even if it weren't his duty. As far as Mr. Holmes and myself well, you must understand. We have been in this business for far too long to take a case and not believe that ultimately there may be danger. We enter into a case prepared for any possible danger, prepared for any possible injury. But that does not stop us. I daresay, anything of that sort will never stop Mr. Holmes. Once he is committed to a case, he is as Berihun. Relentless in his quest to solve it, unwavering in the search for the truth and would give his life if need be to save his charge.

"In that respect, you must understand that we are all alike. In your case, you would do whatever it takes to protect your father and your brother. And whatever led you to put yourself in harm's way today, we must believe that your intention was for the good. One cannot ask any more of another than that, can one?"

Sharrey threw her arms about Watson's neck and hugged him. "Oh, Dr. Watson, you are so kind. I am so happy to have you here."

"Now, you will use the time to change? I shall wait with Miss Rothman and Mr. Mitanni." Watson ducked sheepishly out of the tent, still feeling the warmth of her arms about his neck.

"She will be fine," he said joining them. "I will take her to see Berihun and her father. Berihun has requested them."

"I am so glad she is all right. Oh! Dr. Watson! When I saw her, I thought she was dreadfully hurt!" Minnie cried.

"All superficial thanks to Berihun. That man saved her life once more," Watson said.

"I'm glad he is there for her. And as long as she will be safe in your care, I think I will brave this horrible storm and go to see James. He is not aware of anything that has happened and even though he may not be able to understand, I think I will tell him anyway. Talking always helps and I need to talk," Minnie said.

"That may be just what the doctor ordered, Minnie. It seems James is responding to your visits and that of Sharrey. Perhaps it won't be long to a full recovery. Let us pray for that," Colter said. "I shall walk you to our tent. I know, I know," he held up his hands in defense. "I can see you wish to be alone with James, and I understand that. I will escort you there, then return with Sharrey and Dr. Watson to the infirmary. I wish to hear what Berihun has to say, also."

"I am ready," Sharrey emerged several minutes later. "I apologize to both of you. I was not myself."

Minnie hugged her and smiled. "Don't worry about it, Shar, we understand. While you to go see Berihun, I am going to stay with James. I think that would be good for both of us."

"Are we ready? Pull your shawls up, the wind has not died down much," Watson said.

Colter pulled his collar over his face and together with Minnie Rothman, was thrust by the force of the wind into a half run until they were at James's tent. "Take care of him, Minnie, I will be back shortly." He ushered her inside then hurried to catch up with Watson and Sharrey.

Minnie ran to where James lay. She threw her head on his chest and broke into sobs. "Oh, James! You don't know what just happened!" she cried.

James reached over and caressed her hair. He pushed himself up, pulling Minnie into his arms. He gave a curt thrust of his head to Chibale indicating him to leave them alone. Once Chibale was gone, James held Minnie from him and wiped the tears from her face. "Now my love, what has just happened that has upset you so."

"Oh, James! Sharrey was attacked and nearly killed again! If it hadn't been for Berihun, she would be dead! Oh, James! That wasn't in the plan. You didn't tell me you were going to hurt Sharrey. All you told me was that you wanted the ring and the box. How could you?"

"I have never planned, nor ever will plan to injure Sharrey, Minnie. She is my sister and although I hardly know her, I love her for that. What do you mean, again?"

"James? You mean it. It wasn't you?"

"No Minnie, I would never hurt Sharrey. I know that if I asked her, she would simply give me that box and ring because she does not know their significance. And furthermore, even if she knew, I think if I asked her for them, she would still give them to me. I would never hurt her. Now explain to me this 'again' that you mentioned."

"On the ship coming here, someone put a huge snake, a deadly cobra in her room. It nearly attacked her, but Berihun was able to get hold of the thing and with Mr. Holmes's help, they threw it into the ocean."

"Oh my God!" James exclaimed. "And you think I could do such a thing? Minnie! You must believe me, I would never!"

"I do, I do believe you James. But once more on the boat from Alexandria, someone attacked that boy, Whittingham and hit him on the head. He's just a boy, James. It was then I began to be really afraid. I didn't know what to think. I tried not to believe it was you but then I grew more afraid that if not you then someone else is trying to harm Sharrey and that made me more afraid than ever because she is my best friend in the whole world and I was afraid for her and I couldn't tell her. Oh, James. And now! Someone lured her to the pyramid and tried to kill her with stones. If Berihun hadn't pushed her aside and protected her with his own body, she would have been crushed! James! What are we going to do?" Minnie burst into tears.

James hugged her to him. "I don't know, Minnie. I don't know. But I can tell you honestly, none of that was my doing. I would never hurt Sharrey. Someone else is trying to hurt her."

"But what are we to do? Are we going to tell them about you? Do you think we should?"

"No...no we better not just yet. If it comes out now that I was only pretending, they would cast all the blame on me for these events and perhaps lessen their protection of Sharrey. Besides, I do not wish to be blamed for something I did not do. Wishing to gain control of the ring and the box is one thing, but I would never hurt you or anyone else. You believe me, don't you, my love?"

"Yes I do. I am so relieved I had a chance to speak with you alone. There is so much I want to say. I love having your arms around me, James. When can we give up this charade and tell everyone that you are well and we are in love?"

"Soon...soon, my dear, soon. I think we must keep this charade for a bit longer. Sharrey needs protection still. And I see Sherlock Holmes is here. That is good. Now that Berihun is indisposed, Holmes will see to her protection. If anyone can find out what is going on, he can. He will find the culprit and put a stop to these attacks on her life."

The short walk to the infirmary seemed to take forever. Drifting dunes were mounting, obstructing the path and obliterating travel routes. Colter cleared away the pile at the infirmary door and they entered to find that Professor Princeton and Holmes were sitting silently across from each other with Berihun between them.

"And how is our patient?" Watson queried setting his valise on the table. Relief was evident on Berihun's face when he saw Sharrey. With help from Watson and propped by pillows, he said,

"It is good you are well, my Queen," he bowed his head slightly.

"Stop calling me that!" Sharrey cried. "I do not understand that."

"Please sit and I will tell you then you will understand. But I must have some water first. Then I will begin."

Chapter Twenty

"**I** must begin more than three thousand years ago. It was during the time of the reign of the Pharaoh Snefru. This man was the son of the old Pharaoh Huni. He was not a direct royal heir because he was the son of a minor wife. Because of this he had no claim to the throne unless the true wife had no sons. In this case, there were none and Snefru came to power. Because of this inferior lineage, Snefru married the daughter of Huni, his half sister, Hetepheres, for he wished to further affirm and solidify his position as pharaoh.

"He was young, ambitious and bold. He immediately set about building a pyramid that would become his tomb in the afterlife. The pyramid at the area of Meidum was hindered by a series of events we magi believe to have been caused by the sabotage of those wanting to kill the pharaoh. It was said the pyramid was too large for the steepness of the slopes and it would not hold. It was some time before Snefru relinquished and set new goals for a pyramid at Dashur. He said he was the true son of the gods and that his pyramid, his royal tomb, was more than a stepping stone to the gods. Instead of creating the pyramids in a stepping formation, he decided to build it smooth on all sides. Its height would represent the rise to the sun, and the sun represented the beginning of all things. And because he was the son of the god, he was the beginning of all things.

"In all of his conquests, reaching further into the lands of the Africa and gaining control became his main ambition. He possessed a great military might. His forces invaded as far south as Nubia and the lands to the south of the great Nile River. Nubia brought riches not found in any other region of the continent. Diamonds, emeralds, gold, exotic woods and spices and slaves. Nubia was brimming with everything he wished for his own. What he did not know was that the king of Nubia was a peaceful man and did not wish to see his kingdom destroyed by wars and so offered a truce. Anything the Pharaoh Snefru wished from Nubia, he could have, peacefully, as long as he, King Hashita could maintain the rule over Nubia. He also offered his only daughter, Amanirena, as a peace offering to Snefru and to bind their truce.

"The day came for the great decision and Hashita sent many camels and donkeys bearing the riches of his land for the Egyptian pharaoh. And Snefru was very pleased. Entering the halls at the last was Amanirena. She was very beautiful and proud. Tall and slender, she wore her black hair long and loose down her back, woven with strands of the richest jewels of Nubia. Her black skin had been rubbed with the galbalum oil of her land until it glistened like the black diamond in the torches of the pharaoh's bodyguards. It's aromatic smell enchanted and bewitched all who set eyes upon her beauty. The Pharaoh Snefru was said to have stood and stared mesmerized in awe by her beauty.

"Amanirena was not only the daughter of the king of Nubia, she was also a high priestess of the goddess, Isis. Her beauty and her mystical powers soon had Snefru as her lover and mate. A son was born to them, the first son of the Pharaoh, and he grew happy and content within the royal grounds. But there was jealousy in the heart of his true wife, Hetepheres, for she had not as yet born a son to her husband. When the boy was but three years old he was poisoned. It was never proven, but we, the magi, believed it to be the work of Hetepheres, for with no son for her throne that of Amanirena would be first in line.

"Soon Amanirena was again with child and the hatred of Queen Heterpheres was no long hidden. Pharaoh Snefru appointed three of his most trusted magi to protect her. But Heterpheres was not to be undone. Once more, the child, another son, was found dead only months after his birth and Snefru grew angry with rage. It was but through the love of Amanirena that he was able to forgive. She convinced him to sleep with Heterpheres until she was with child and that he did. But not only did she conceive, so did Amanirena a third time. The Pharaoh, believing her child once more to be a male heir, grew more and more fearful for her life.

"Alone in his chambers one evening, he gave to Amanirena the ring made of diamonds and emeralds inscribed with his love for her, and her alone, and vowed that there would always be peace between his kingdom and Nubia. She in turn gave him the black box hand carved from the wood of the black ebony and inscribed with her love for him and the protection of her goddess Isis for her lover for as long as peace remained.

"The Pharaoh then had his three magi take Amanirena away to a far distant land where they were ordered to protect not only her, but her child and the children of the children until the end of the ages and to take the ring and the box which decreed the symbol of their love for each other, for the promises of peace to each other. Amanirena had a daughter and all the daughters since had had daughters and we, the magi, have been protecting these daughters of the daughters of the Queen for these long centuries.

"The magic of the ring and the box is misunderstood. Ownership of them does not give the owner control over people or riches. The riches become the word used to symbolize the love of the king for his queen and she for him. For when one has love, there are no greater riches in the world than that. The control over the people was symbolic of their profession of the peace that would always exist between their nations. It is in this that whoever has the ring and the box would speak through the true and rightful blood line of the Pharaoh Snefru and Queen Amanirena and there would always be a growing love and peace between the nations."

"But how would we even begin to know who the true and rightful blood line would be?" Sharrey asked.

"Do you not experience strange sensations when you wear the ring?" Berihun asked.

"Yes, but I do not like it at all," she said.

"It will not harm you. It is the spirit of Queen Amanirena speaking through the ages to you. It is she telling you what you must do to bring about the peace back to Egypt and Nubia for once she was removed from this land, war broke out and there has been struggle and death ever since."

"But how does that explain Dr. Watson?"

"What is this?" Berihun turned to Watson.

"Well, it appears that whenever I grasp the box I experience the same sensations as Miss Princeton when she wears the ring. How do you explain that, my good man?" Watson asked.

"It is simple," Berihun smiled. "The spirit of the Pharaoh Snefru speaks to you through the box, telling you that love for one another must be restored before the peace and freedom can be gained once more between Egypt and Nubia."

"But that is absurd! That would mean…the blood line…how absurd!" Watson sputtered.

"And why should that be so, Dr. Watson? Do you know your heritage of the past three thousand years?"

"Why no! That would be impossible for anyone to know that!" Watson cried.

"Would it? I can tell you my heritage. I can tell you in truth of Miss Princeton's heritage. She is the daughter of Queen Sari Nefrati, who was the daughter of Queen Nasala, the daughter of Queen Qalhata, going all the way back to Queen Amanirena. We, the magi, have protected these queens for three thousand years. We have protected the ring and the box for three thousand years. And now, we have a true blood line to our Queen ready to accept the responsibility of the ring and a true blood line to the Pharaoh to accept the responsibility of the box."

"But, that's preposterous! I could no longer be heir to that box of Egypt than…than...to the crown of England!" Watson sputtered.

"Shall we put it to the test," Holmes said. He pulled the ring and box from his pocket.

"*No*!" Shouted Watson. "I will not touch that box!"

"But Dr. Watson, if what Berihun says is true, then we have an obligation, a promise to keep. A promise of ages. We will not know if we do not try. I am willing to put the ring back on if you are willing to hold the box," Sharrey put a gentle hand to Watson's arm. "Please! Don't we owe it to these people?"

Watson stared from one expectant face to another around the room. Holmes pulled the chair close and said, "Here, old man. Sit down and take the box. We will all be here if or when it must be removed from your grasp. If the lady is willing?"

Sharrey sat opposite Dr. Watson. She reached for the ring that Holmes was holding out to her and put it on her finger and with her other hand, took Watson's in hers. Watson closed his eyes for a long moment and let out his breath. Holding the gentle, comforting hand of Sharrey Princeton in his, a sudden feeling of warmth and safety came over him and he reached for the box.

Chapter Twenty-One

Almost immediately the feeling of being over powered swept over them both. The room swirled into a mist and all else in the room became blurred. Events of ancient history passed before them, rising through the mist to crystal clarity to be swept away and replaced by others. It began thousands of years ago, the vision of Snefru lying with his beloved Amanirena on a dais in the shade of a palm tree overlooking the construction of the pyramid at Dashur. A man and woman truly in love. The loss of their sons, Amonoa and Imea, their names swept from history by the envious treachery of Hetepheres. Amanirena hustled away from Snefru's kingdom in the dark of the night, her hand clutching tight to the child she carried in her womb.

The visions of succeeding kingdoms swept past, kingdoms of Egypt and Nubia now at war, king fighting king, villages destroyed, peopled murdered or enslaved. Great dams built to curb the flow of the Nile and the domination of Egypt by the king of Nubia, Shabaka who brought prosperity to Egypt, enhancing the temples at Memphis and Abydos in honor of the gods who favored him greatly. The grievous loss of kingship of Egypt to the Ottoman Empire, the bloody revolts and deaths in the take over by the French and an ever growing anger rising throughout the peoples of Egypt while the government was being overtaken and the land ravaged by the British.

And throughout was the whispering of Pharaoh Snefru, of his love for Amanirena, his profession of peace for the lands of Egypt and Nubia. The soft, throaty voice of Amanirena vowing her love for Snefru, calling upon the goddess Isis to protect her lover for she was the giver of life. The spirit of love and peace, of calm and serenity, of hope and freedom circled and encompassed Sharrey and Watson until, with the passage of the visions of time, the swirling mist disappeared and they were brought to look at each other once more and those around them came into clarity.

The room was silent. Nothing stirred for even the howling wind had ceased. When vision cleared, Watson looked into Sharrey Princeton's eyes and a great sigh came from them both. Sharrey smiled at Watson. "We have survived the ordeal and come through with nothing but knowledge, Dr. Watson," she whispered.

"Yes. It was unlike the past with the strange sensations, the fainting and the headaches. Somehow it was different this time," he said.

"Perhaps it was because we were together, holding hands like Snefru and Amanirena did. Perhaps that is what is needed to help bring peace to this Africa. A holding of hands, an understanding of others, a realization that we are not all alike and should be allowed to be free individuals."

"Perhaps we ask too much," Watson whispered back.

"Whatever we ask, Dr. Watson," Berihun said to them, "we now know you are both direct blood decendents of our King and Queen."

"But I am not interested in this affair. I am not from this country," Watson sputtered once more. "There is nothing I can do to help."

"We shall see," Berihun smiled. "We shall see."

Whittingham burst into the tent coming to a teetering halt for he was taken by surprise at the silence that engulfed the room. "Mr. Holmes, is everything all right?"

"Everything is just fine, Whittingham. What is it you need?"

"Nothing, sir. I just wanted to let everyone know that the storm has stopped as suddenly as it started and that the workers are setting to cleaning away the sand and some of them have a meal prepared, sir. They…they sent me to tell you, that's all."

"Good. After all this I am ravenous, are you not, Watson?" Holmes clapped his friend on the shoulder.

"Actually, I am rather hungry. But Berihun, I must…"

"No, you must get yourself a good meal. I shall stay while Whittingham here goes to set food to a tray and bring it back here for him," Holmes said.

"But the animals, sir. After all this storm, I must make sure they are watered and cleaned and…but I will go fetch that tray, Mr. Holmes," Whittingham raced from the tent.

Holmes broke into laughter and patted Watson once more on the back. "That boy is good to have around, Watson. Very happy we decided to keep the lad. I am thinking that Berihun does not need our assistance as long as he promises to stay in bed. We will see to Miss Princeton, eh Berihun?"

"I will stay, I give my word. I would not ordinarily admit this, but I truly feel terrible." Everyone laughed at his embarrassed remark. He continued. "But now that I have shared my story and everyone knows the truth, I am much relieved. It is much easier to complete a task when one knows what the circumstances are and what is expected of him." Already, Whittingham was returning with a tray. Beneath the cloth were mounds of bread and a large bowl of steaming chunks of meat swimming in a rich savory broth and several bowls of fresh dates and figs along with a pitcher of water. Berihun reached to pull the tray closer.

Chapter Twenty-Two

The storm abated, the wind curbed its wrathful fury weakening to a gentle breeze that was welcomed. They sat at the long table outside and chatted and laughed easily over the evening meal.

"After the ordeal of today this table setting looks like a feast!" Sharrey smiled. "Thank you all," she said to the women who bowed to her, pleased that she was happy.

"It certainly does. And I am famished," Minnie said reaching to fill her plate.

"Why Minnie, are you beginning to like Egypt?" Sharrey asked.

"Oh, don't be absurd," she quickly replied.

"Father, do you think after the meal we might be able to go down to your dig site?" Sharrey asked.

"I don't see why not. But wouldn't you wish to rest, my dear. After all, you have just been through a terrible ordeal."

"I really would like to see the work you do, Father. Now that I am aware of the history of this place, I would like to learn more from you. I feel that the more I can learn now, the easier it will be when I must fulfill my obligations to my heritage."

"Very well said, Miss Princeton," Watson said. "But, as far as my part in this historic event is concerned, I do not feel that I am in any way, shape or form, Egyptian, despite the blood line Berihun speaks of. I do not feel that

201

I could or would, for that matter, be able to do justice to the situation."

Holmes said, "I propose an arrangement."

"Arrangement? Of what sort?" Watson queried.

"We must speak to Berihun before making this arrangement, but perhaps you could, say, appoint a proxy to stand in your stead. One who is Egyptian born, loves the land, knows its history, and is willing to work alongside Miss Princeton to achieve the goals set by the old pharaoh and his queen."

"And you just happen to have someone in mind?" Princeton asked.

"I do," Holmes turned his attention to Colter Mitanni.

"Me! You can't possibly mean me?" Mitanni protested.

"Why not?" Holmes shrugged. "We are all aware of your heritage, your reputation as a distinguished archeologist, thus knowing more than anyone of the history of the country. You have traveled widely and have a working knowledge of the people and the situations that abound here. You are Egyptian, you love the country and furthermore you are in love with Miss Princeton, which would make you the perfect proxy for Dr. Watson."

"I…I," Colter sputtered,

"Oh, Colter, would you? Could you?" Sharrey took his hand in hers. "Mr. Holmes is right and there is no sense in denying our feelings for each other or for this country. I know how hard I will work to achieve the goals of peace for this country, and I know how hard you would work to achieve those goals with me. What else is there to say?"

Those sitting around the table waited expectantly. Looking from face to face unaware of the chunk of bread he had dipped into the broth and held to his mouth, Mitanni stammered, "I …I believe you have cornered me, Mr. Holmes. I have only one thing to say...perhaps two. Yes, I would consider it an honor to be proxy for Dr. Watson, if he would have me, for Egypt is my home and I will do whatever it takes to bring back the peace of my people. And second, yes, Sharrey. you are correct also in my feelings not only for this land but also for you and I cannot think there is anything further to do but to ask you to marry me."

"Oh yes! Yes! I will certainly marry you!" Sharrey threw her arms about his neck, laughing when the gravied bread stuck to her elbow.

"My goodness," Peter Princeton sighed. "What a strange turn of events this day has brought! It seems so much has happened and I appear to be the one left in the dark. Sharrey! Colter! I was not aware of your feelings for each other. But I will say congratulations with my blessings. I could not wish for a more loving and caring man to give my daughter to in marriage."

"Oh Father, thank you!"

"What say you, Watson, to Colter as your proxy then we can get down to the business of eating," Holmes said.

"It would be my pleasure to accept Colter. It would be my pleasure to dig into this meal as I too, am starving!" Watson laughed.

"Good! Then after we will take that walk to the dig site," Professor Princeton said.

They followed him down the path weaving around the wreckage of the stone wall and rounded the next bend. It was here they were forced to stop. Not only had the wall collapsed, but the entire path to the pyramid had been obliterated.

"Now what are we to do?" Sharrey asked.

"Not much we can do, my dear. It will take several days for the workmen to clear this giving us access to the pyramid. We may be able to go around but it will be a much longer walk."

"Then let's go," Minnie said. "After all this talk about pharaohs and pyramids and tombs, I am anxious to see it for myself."

"Me too," Sharrey agreed. "I don't mind the walk, Father. The walk will do us good."

"Then let's get to it, shall we?" Princeton led them on. He circled around for several feet saying, "Many times after such a storm, the sand settles hard enough for us to walk upon, but I do not wish to take any chances. You will follow single file and step in my tracks very carefully. Sometimes the sand shifts from the weight."

"Father! This is the dig site? The pyramid of Snefru?" Sharrey exclaimed when the pyramid came into view. Much of the stone had been removed and the theft of its outer casing left the Red Pyramid looking coarse and fragmented.

"This is it, my dear, his second attempt, so history tells us. The other is further down there. But if you all look up, there just about twenty to thirty feet, you will see the entrance to the pyramid. We had cleared a path up and once we breached the entrance we constructed a metal door for security reasons, you see. More from tomb raiders than sand, but I am happy in this instance, it has protected our corridors from filling up once more."

"But if the pyramid was sealed, there shouldn't be any debris, should there?" Minnie asked.

"Not if it had been an intact tomb, Miss Rothman. Once the beliefs in the old religions were replaced with such as Christianity and Islam, there were those people who began to break into the pyramids, raid the tombs of the old pharaohs, steal the artifacts and sell them on the black market. We have discovered many such tombs and the loss of the stolen artifacts is incalculable. They have dug holes, desecrated the mummies, laying to waste and ruin the priceless beauty of the ancient kingdoms; a sacrilege to the old religions to be sure."

"But I don't understand, what gives anyone the right to come to this land and take what isn't theirs?" Sharrey said angrily. "These pyramids and all they hold belong to the people of Egypt. Others have no right to take them. It is …well…it is stealing."

"Then I am to understand that you don't agree with the archeological work of your father, Miss Princeton? After all most if not all of the artifacts he finds are shipped elsewhere," Holmes remarked.

"Is this true, Father?" Sharrey asked. "Then this must stop. It must stop immediately. If Colter and I are to attempt to bring the nations of Africa together in peace, we must start by giving them back their heritage. Give them back what is rightfully theirs."

"You do not understand, my dear. There have been so much of these ancient sites that have been discovered, their entire contents have been strewn to every part of the globe, public and private. To bring them back would be a huge undertaking, not to mention impossible to accomplish!" Princeton exclaimed. "I do agree it must be stopped. And from here on, I will see to it that all my discoveries will be turned over to the proper authorities in antiquities in Egypt."

"That will be one of the first steps we try to accomplish, Sharrey. Convince the government that these historical monuments must be preserved. That all antiquities from the ancients must be returned and displayed in Egypt as our heritage," Colter said.

"Yes, I agree a viable solution is needed," Sharrey said. "But that is for later and right now I would like to see inside. May we Father?"

"Of course, come this way, watch your step. The walkway has been made unsteady by the storm so proceed with caution."

"And here we are," Princeton extracted a set of keys and unlocked the door. It was their first glimpse into the pyramid.

"Oh! It's black as pitch in there!" Minnie exclaimed.

"Yes," Princeton laughed, "which is why we have the torches placed just inside here. Help yourself to one and we'll go inside."

They crept along a low ceilinged corridor that sloped down at an angle until it opened into a large chamber approximately fifteen feet wide. Figures of people and animals as well as the hieroglyphic writings were carved on the stone, painted in bright colors that, after all the centuries, remained undamaged. The ceiling stretched above their heads, each succeeding tier of stone overlapping the previous by mere inches until the entire complex came together at the top, called a corbel roof. In this way, each tier of stone interlocked with the next creating a solid and stable platform for the remainder of the pyramid to be built upon.

"Here to your left you will see the first burial chamber," Princeton said.

"There…there aren't any mummies in there, are there?" Minnie asked.

"No my dear, everything from this pyramid has been raided and stolen years ago. It is such a shame. Nothing from the Pharaoh Snefru has ever been discovered except for these empty tombs. The reason we know these belong to Snefru is the writing on the walls. They tell of a great pharaoh, his battles, his pyramids and his ascension into the afterlife to live as the god he proclaimed to be, once his body had died. His tombs must have contained many beautiful artifacts for this was a great pharaoh," Princeton said.

"What a shame," Sharrey murmured.

"But you do have the ring and the box, Professor," Watson said. "Are these not from the Pharaoh Snefru?"

"Yes they are, but they are two of the most sacred artifacts of all time and they cannot be brought to light just yet," Princeton said.

"But then why do you still dig here, Father. If there is nothing left, why do you dig?"

"Sari told me long ago that Snefru was never the same once Amanirena was gone. He longed for her company, missed her goodness and beauty but he was also afraid of what might happen should she return. Once Hetepheres had produced an heir to his kingdom, he secretly sent word through the magi to bring Amanirena back. Which they did. But she was not well. The birth of her daughter was too much for her. When Snefru called her back to join him, she left her daughter in hiding with the three magi and returned alone. She was not here for very long when she died in his arms.

"There was a rumor that his Bent Pyramid further down the path, was left unfinished because it was considered unsafe due to the angle. This is not true. The true reason, according to Sari, was that when Amanirena died Snefru secretly had her mummy buried there. He purposefully had the angle altered, a sign of the sorrow of his broken heart. He discarded the pyramid as his own tomb probably starting the rumors himself so the burial of Amanirena would not be discovered.

"It was said that Snefru's love for her was so great, that the Bent Pyramid was actually planned to be her resting place all along. This Red Pyramid, as it has become known, was to be his. He was going to be sure they would be together in the afterlife if they could not be in this mortal life. There is only a mile separating the two pyramids as you can see. There are supposed to be connecting corridors between the two pyramids. The corridors have niches with statues of themselves placed there so that should their tombs be raided, at least they could still be with each other through their statuary. But as yet, to date, nothing has been found either in the Red Pyramid or the Bent pyramid, the reason why I will never stop looking."

"Oh Father! You have been searching for Mother's ancestors all these years?"

"Yes, don't you see? I thought that if I could find the mummies of Snefru and Amanirena and bring them together, the legends of the ring and the box would be fulfilled and your involvement need never come to light. There would once again be peace in Africa and I could rest assured that you would always be safe. I know, here in my heart, Sharrey, that they will be together and there will be peace."

"Oh Father!" Sharrey put her arms about his neck and kissed his cheek. "I did not know how much you loved her, how deep was your adoration for her. But I can see it now, Father. I only wish you had allowed me to be a part of this all along. I would have helped. I would have done anything for I am sure Mother is watching and guiding you from the afterlife."

"Thank you, my dear. She would be so proud of you, as am I," Princeton declared.

"We should be getting back. It's getting late and very dark," Colter said.

"Yes of course," Princeton said. "We shall finish our examination of the pyramid once the workers have cleared out pathway."

"Then I think tomorrow we should go to Dashur. We could thank the women who decorated our tent and do some shopping," Minnie suggested.

"Excellent idea," Princeton agreed.

Chapter Twenty-Three

The following morning Minnie yawned and called out to Sharrey. "Are you ready to visit Dashur today?"

"Oh, I nearly forgot about going today."

Minnie laughed. "No need to rush. I am just getting up myself. I plan to visit the whole city and simply enjoy myself."

"Me too, but first we must thank the women who created our hideaway here. It is so beautiful."

"Yes we must and once that's done we will shop and enjoy the rest of the day and let the men worry about everything else."

"I rather like that," Sharrey said.

"So are you two ladies ready for Dashur?" Colter asked.

"The question is, my good sir, is Dashur ready for us?" Minnie giggled.

"Might I make a suggestion?" Princeton spoke up. "It would be easier for you to take the small craft from the jetty up the river to the city. It is much quicker than walking the distance in the heat."

Mitanni said. "I'm sure we are all in agreement on that."

They ate quickly and soon they set out for the jetty. Whittingham brought up the rear with Queenie following close at hand. There were always several small crafts tied to the jetty with one flat bottomed barge that was large enough to transport animals if necessary. There were also several young boys, not old enough to work at the pyramids but too old to not work at all, who manned the crafts between the city and the dig site.

Watson eyed the small watercraft already over-crowded. "Holmes, I do hope you don't mind but I will take the barge with Whittingham and Queenie. I was able to inventory the medical supplies in the infirmary and found them to be deficient. I will be spending my time acquiring the supplies needed not only for the infirmary here but also to replenish those in my valise."

"Not at all, Watson," Holmes replied.

"We shall see you back at the dig site later then," Watson called to them.

The small craft was quickly set to by young workers and it wasn't long before they neared the long and narrow jetty on the outskirts of Dashur.

"You will find Dashur an old city," Colter said. "It was built thousands of years ago probably when the pharaoh's workmen came to build the pyramids. It has lasted the test of time, although it has altered locations many times due to the changing course of the Nile throughout the years. It is a good place for a city. It is sheltered at the rear by the sandstone cliffs that protect it somewhat from the howling storms of the desert. It has all the advantages of the Nile, what with the shipping that passes through the area and the fertile deposits that arrive each year with the annual inundation of the Nile. The people have constructed canals skirting the city that bring in water from the Nile not only for agriculture, but also for their daily consumption as well. It is a good place for a city. Ah, here we are, first to the market place where I will introduce you to the woman responsible for your accommodations."

The city was a cluster of shops and houses, the streets were narrow and crude, every inch filled with vendors and their goods. All around was the constant crying of vendors. The smell of fresh baked breads, cooking meats and frying vegetables permeated the air.

"Here we are," Mitanni stopped at a narrow stall filled with intricately woven blankets. "This is the carpet stall of Aisha Alima, the wife of Maraq. She takes great pride in her work and is known throughout the entire region as having the best quality of dyed cottons and superior weaving."

A woman emerged from the dark room behind the stall and Colter bowed, putting his hand to his chest, a symbolic greeting in Dashur. Aisha Alima, wife of Iqbal Maraq, I have brought to you Miss Sharrey Princeton and her good friend Miss Minerva Rothman. This gentlemen is Mr. Sherlock Holmes who has accompanied Miss Princeton safely from England."

Sharrey bowed, following Colter's lead and said, "My friend and I wish to thank you and all the women who have decorated our tent. My father, Peter Princeton, has told us of your insistence and we are so grateful. Your work is extremely beautiful!"

Aisha Alima bowed and went quickly to her knees. "My Queen, I am but a humble servant and not worthy of your praise! It is the pleasure of the women of Dashur and myself to have provided such elegance for you, my Queen. We have known of your heritage and have waited many years for your return to take your rightful place among the queens of Egypt."

Sharrey exclaimed. "Please get up! How do you know of this?"

Aisha Alima bowed once more. "Do not fear that we know," she continued. "There are many of us here in Dashur that have stayed with the old ways and customs. There are many of us here who still believe in the legends and yes, the curses of the pharaohs of old. We know and understand that such things can come true. And this must be so, for here you are at last. We have waited a long time for this day."

"I don't know what to say," Sharrey stuttered.

"Say no more. Your presence has already raised the hope in us all. More than you can ever know. Know that we are with you and will do as you bid," Aisha Alima finally rose then bowed once more.

"Well…well, thank you," Sharery said bewildered.

"Thank you," Colter said. "We will take up no more of your time. Good day."

"The peace of all the gods of Egypt and Nubia go with you," and Aisha Alima was gone.

"That was certainly strange," Minnie said

"It is their way," Colter said. "The people here do not require over much praise. They seem to know when a person is genuine and they accept that. I am afraid you have a lot to live up to, Sharrey."

"I can see that. I don't know if I am up to that. I don't know if I can live up to the expectations of all these people."

"They don't expect much, Sharrey. They just expect you to do your best. After all you are the direct blood descendent of the Pharaoh Snefru and Queen Amanirena and only good can come of that," Colter said.

"Well, I've had enough of this queen stuff and pharaoh stuff. Let's do some shopping!" exclaimed Minnie.

Chapter Twenty-Four

"Thank you, Whittingham, for staying behind with me. I know how much you wished to see the city," Watson said. "But we will need the services of that Queenie of yours. The supplies are sorely depleted back at the infirmary."

"That is all right, Dr. Watson. Here, let me help you onto the barge. No need to worry about Queenie. She will follow on her own accord." Watson stepped onto the swaying barge and Queenie, true to Whittingham's word, followed an unspoken command and diligently followed. Once loaded, the Egyptian youth hoisted the pole and shoved off from the jetty. He skillfully pulled the pole hand over hand pushing off the bottom of the Nile, guiding them along the river bank until they bumped against the jetty near Dashur. The small craft carrying the first party had arrived some time earlier and were nowhere to be seen.

"Grab Queenie's rope there boy, for there are many distractions here and we would hate to have her wander off."

"I will." Whittingham secured the donkey, looked around and asked, "Where do we go from here?"

"I say we follow the road there and perhaps we will run into someone who can direct us to the clinic here."

With the rope slung loosely over Whittingham's shoulder they set off. Every so often Watson saw the boy reach in his pocket and giving the donkey something to munch which piqued Watson's interest.

"What have you there, lad?"

"They are dried grapes, Dr. Watson. Some of the boys that work at clearing at the pyramid told me of these. They take the grapes and put them on the tops of stones to dry. Once they are dried, they shrivel up to these little things here," Whittingham held his hand out to show Watson. "They said they last forever and are a staple for the caravans that spend days traveling through the deserts from town to town. They taste pretty good. Want to try some? Queenie just loves them." He popped several in his mouth.

"They are rather good," Watson said munching on several of the dried fruit. "It is no wonder the animals follow you everywhere. You have tricked them."

"No, I do not consider it a trick, Dr. Watson. I call it training. These little fellows know that I will take care of them and when they are especially good, I give them treats."

"And what has Queenie done especially good today?"

"She came along. I didn't have to tell her or pull on her rope or hit her with a stick like I see others do. She knows I have the dried grapes in my pockets and she just follows. It's as simple as that."

"You are a wonder, young Whittingham," Watson laughed. "Ah, here we are. Civilization."

They reached the top of a small rise and the city of Dashur came into view in the distance, Houses and shops rose out of the desert, built into the steep cliff sides that rose behind it.

"Oh my!" Whittingham exclaimed.

Taken in by the simple beauty of it, they were unaware of the old man hobbling along the narrow path until he spoke. "Your donkey for sale?" he reached out for the rope.

"No!" Whittingham shouted. "She's mine, no! She's not for sale!"

The old man drew back. "I meant no disrespect."

"Say, perhaps you can help us," Watson said. "Can you point us in the direction of the clinic. The clinic? Doctors?"

"Doctora, yes, yes," the old man nodded and pointed in the direction from which they had just come. "Go to first road on right and turn. That is all." The old man eyed Queenie once more. He shook his head dolefully, hefted his weighty load and shuffled off down the path.

"That man frightened me, Dr. Watson. I thought he was going to grab at Queenie."

"He might have, but the situation was avoided. You do not know the people nor their customs, Whittingham. Best keep a tight hold on that rope."

"I will, sir. Don't you fret my Queenie girl. You are safe with me and Dr. Watson." Whittingham stroked the donkey's forehead and she nuzzled his pocket for more dried grapes. They set off once more, turning where the old man had indicated. The sun was rising hot and fiery and Whittingham retrieved two straw hats from Queenie's pack. "They are crude but I am just learning how to weave them," the boy said.

"They will do just fine. Just fine indeed," Watson said. It was a short distance before he saw the clinic in the distance. It was an old structure, the coat of diluted whitewash faded over the weathered boards. The steps sagged and the screen door flapped freely in the wind, hanging on by one rusted hinge.

"I can understand why Professor Princeton chose to keep his son at the dig site," Whittingham muttered when they entered.

"Hello!" Watson called out. "Hello! Is anyone there?" A chair creaked somewhere in the back and a moment later a man appeared in the doorway.

"Hello yourself. Can I help you?" the old man inquired. Standing not much taller than Whittingham, the faded gray eyes peered at them through thick spectacles perched at the end of his nose. "Can I help you?" he asked once more.

"Yes, I am Dr. John Watson and my colleague Whittingham here. We have come from the dig site of Professor Princeton and are in need of replenishing our medical supplies. We were hoping you could help. But perhaps," Watson looked around, "perhaps we ask too much. It appears that your clinic needs more help than we do."

The old man laughed heartily. "Don't be fooled by these accommodations, Dr. Watson. Follow me, back here is the true clinic. We are in the finishing stages of our new accommodations and have not yet had the time to tear down the old." He led them through the doorway down a narrow hall where he stepped through into the new clinic.

"We run a tight ship here as you can see. What can I help you with? I'm afraid our shipment of supplies is not due for several more weeks, but we can give you what we are able."

"Thank you, I appreciate your help. I have a list here, some are for the infirmary back at the dig site and some I need for my own valise, if you don't mind."

"Not at all, follow me to the supply room and we shall see what we have for you."

"Whittingham, I can take care of this. Why don't you go back and stay with Queenie."

"I will sir. I will see you there." Whittingham bounded out of the clinic and led Queenie to the shaded side of the building where he leaned back and waited for Watson. He jumped up quickly when he saw Watson returning. "Got everything, Dr. Watson?"

"As much as the good Dr. O'Hallahan was able to provide. Load a box to each side of Queenie and we must be off. It will be late by the time we get back but we are in luck. The good doctor has provided us with a sandwich and a jug of water for the way back."

They had traveled back for some distance before Whittingham stopped Queenie.

"Dr. Watson?"

"Yes?"

"There…well, there is something I really have to tell you."

"Go on."

"About me, sir. There's something I really have to tell you about me."

"You mean that you are an orphan, stowed away on the *Sunda* and lied about it?"

The boy's eyes rounded. "You knew! You knew all along?"

"Nearly all along. Holmes and I agreed to keep you on until we returned to London. Then we would try to find a place for you to fit in. You are talented in many areas, young lad," Watson smiled at the boy.

"Mr. Holmes knows, too? You never let on! You have been so kind to me I …I don't know what to say. I wanted to tell you, but I was afraid you would send me back or worse yet, turn me over to the police when we reached land."

"We would never have done that, Whittingham. That's just not Holmes's way."

They continued on until they reached the crossroad where once more Whittingham stopped and spoke.

"Dr. Watson?"

"Yes?"

"There's something else I really have to tell you."

"Yes?"

"Professor Princeton has asked me to stay. He says that I am a natural with the animals and that I have been considerable help to Maraq with the supplies and inventory. He said I could stay and be his assistant. Can you believe it, Dr. Watson? Professor Princeton's assistant?"

"And you wish to stay?"

"Oh yes!" Whittingham exclaimed. "More than anything in the world! I...I mean ...don't think that I don't appreciate all that you and Mr. Holmes have done for me, but I cannot remain a burden on you any longer. This offer from Mr. Princeton is such a great opportunity. He says if I stay, he will hire a tutor for me so I can finish my schooling. He says I must else I would be no good to him in the future."

"And so you have made up your mind and decided to stay."

"Yes, oh yes, I love this land called Egypt!"

"Then that is all we need to know," Watson smiled. "See here, Whittingham. Do not fret over mine or Mr. Holmes's feelings. We are satisfied that you will be under the care and guidance of Professor Princeton. And the fact that it is your wish, adds to the benefits, I daresay. I am happy for you. Ah, here we are at the barge. Let's get loaded and be on our way."

It wasn't until they reached the landing that Watson took notice of the weather. Clouds were slowly filling the sky crushing the sun into veiled obscurity. Watson shuddered sensing a dreaded gloom descending on Egypt.

"Looks like we may be getting a storm," Watson remarked.

"I hope it's not one of those sandstorms again. But I think this one looks like rain."

"Certainly does so we'd best make haste."

"Come on, Queenie, we don't want these medical supplies to get ruined."

"No we would not. Lead the way young man, Lead...."

"What is it Dr. Watson?" Whittingham looked up for neither he nor Watson had been aware of the men who now blocked their path.

"What is it you want?" Watson called out to them, stepping back. But he knew immediately something was wrong. The men did not answer and when several of them roughly took hold of Watson he shouted, "Stay behind Whittingham! Run! Run for help!"

He struggled to get away only then seeing that his words were too late. Whittingham had charged in and jumped on the back of one of the assailants, his thin arm tight against the man's throat. The attacker released his hold on Watson and reached behind grabbing the boy by the scruff of the collar tossing him to the ground, knocking the wind out of him.

Whittingham rolled, shaking the dust from his face tackling the man around the knees while the other three had once more grabbed Watson. They held him fast, beating him until one man pulled out a gun and brought it smashing down on Watson's head. The last thing he saw before crumbling to the ground was one of them hitting Whittingham across the face... then everything went black.

"Bind his hands and feet. We will leave him in the red to die," one of the men grunted, wiping blood from his face.

"What of the boy?"

"Gag and tie him to his donkey. We will send him back to this Sherlock Holmes with a message." the first ,said.

Whittingham's arms were pulled back and his hands tied tightly with rope. A dirty piece of cloth was tied around his mouth. He was thrust on Queenie's back and one of the men grabbed him by the front of the shirt. "You hear me, boy?" he growled. "You give a message to that Sherlock Holmes. You tell him to go home. Go back to London and leave this place. This is not his war. If he does not leave, his man Watson will die. You tell him this, yes?"

Whittingham was petrified. Watson was there, lying bleeding and unconscious in the sand. The man jerked his collar thrusting his face inches from the boy. "You tell him this, yes?"

Whittingham nodded vigorously, nearly in tears. The man laughed and slapped Queenie on the rump. With a frightened bawl, she scurried out of their way, heading straight for home.

Chapter Twenty-Five

"**W**here the devil is Watson? What could be keeping the man?" Holmes asked for the third time. "It is nearly dark and there is a storm brewing. They should have been back hours ago. They were only getting supplies!"

"Relax, Mr. Holmes. I am sure they were out enjoying the sites of Dashur and forgot the time," Minnie said.

"No, this is unlike Watson. He is a single-minded individual. If he set out to get supplies, he would have done just that," Holmes said.

"But.." Princeton began, interrupted by the cries and shouts in the distance. "Ah, he is coming. I told you everything would be all right, Mr. Holmes."

Holmes hurried to the group that had assembled.

"It is just a donkey, Effendi, but we go fetch," one of the workmen pointed then went to retrieve the animal. He returned leading Queenie, Whittingham still tied to her back.

"Damn it all!" Holmes cursed reaching for the boy, tearing the gag from his mouth. "Bring a knife! Cut those ties from his hands. They are already raw and bleeding!" He scooped Whittingham off the donkey and started for the infirmary. "Boy! What happened! Where is Watson!"

"For goodness sake, Mr. Holmes, give him some water and let him get his wits about him. Can't you see he's been beaten!" cried Sharrey.

"Fetch the wretched water!" Holmes shouted over his shoulder.

The boy's eyes fluttered open and for several long seconds he was unaware where he was. He was on a cot...there was Berihun...there was Sherlock Holmes staring at him, concern etched in the furrowed brows. Whittingham remembered! He jumped up shouting, "They took him, Mr. Holmes! They took Dr. Watson!"

"Hold on there, boy," Holmes gripped his shoulders. "Who took him? What happened?"

"Men! There were four men at the landing when we were coming back. Their faces were covered...I...I could not see who they were. They attacked us, Mr. Holmes. They beat Dr. Watson really bad. He was hurt and they tied him up and..."

"Oh Whittingham, you poor boy!" cried Sharrey.

"He's not a boy!" Holmes shouted at her. "Step back and let men do their job. Now, Whittingham, calm down and take a deep breath. There. I apologize for my behavior but ...it's Watson. Tell me again. Tell me exactly what happened."

Whittingham took a deep breath and recounted the incident at the landing. "Did they say anything? Anything at all?" Holmes asked.

"They told me to tell you...tell you to leave. That this isn't your war. That you should go home to England. That if you don't, they will kill Dr. Watson! Oh, Mr. Holmes, I tried to help, really I did!" cried Whittingham.

Holmes placed an arm about the boy's shoulder. "You did your best. A man can't ask for more. But think. Is there anything, anything you may have forgotten?"

Whittingham wiped his face and winced at the pain from a cut there, a cut he barely felt when the man hit him and the ring he wore dug through his skin. The wound had crusted over but cracked open once again, the blood trickling down the boy's cheek. He absently wiped at it, his mind rethinking every detail, every second of the attack, every possible piece of information that he may have missed. "Yes...I...I heard one of them say they were going to toss him in the red and let him die."

"In the red?" Sharrey cried. "What is that supposed to mean?"

"In the red...in the red," Holmes mumbled to himself.

"In the red! Of course! The Red Pyramid!" Colter cried. "It has to be!"

"Good man!" Holmes exclaimed "Good man, indeed. We will begin a search immediately. And you, Whittingham, have done well. Watson will be proud."

"Give me a few minutes, sir, and I will be ready to join the search party."

"Oh no you won't," cried Sharrey. "You will stay put and Minnie and I will take care of that wound of yours."

"But I..."

"No lad, Miss Princeton is right. You have been most helpful. You stay with Berihun and rest. We may need your help later," Holmes said. "Right now, there is one more thing I must do."

Chapter Twenty-Six

Watson groaned and a searing pain gripped his head. He lay that way for several long minutes, unable to focus, struggling to breathe, bound hand and foot and unable to move. The sound of his labored breathing echoed around him The air felt threatening, as though an evil lurked in the darkness. Terror gripped him.

The stone beneath his head was cold and he could feel its chill seeping into his very bones. The vision of an attack floated in and out of focus until he remembered Whittingham lying on the ground bleeding. And then it all came back. Whittingham! The poor boy had only just realized his life coming together only to have it snatched away from him by those ruffians. Watson groaned again at the loss.

And Holmes? By God, what would Holmes do? He forced himself to relax, to lie still and think. Get your bearings, he told himself. Slow your breathing and relax. Staring into the darkness, he tried to recalled the definition of darkness. In scientific theory darkness was the absence of light yet even in the darkest recesses, there remained a feeble grayness giving hope to a clarity beyond. That is, of course, unless one is so far beneath the surface of light that a hint of clarity cannot penetrate.

He found that his arms and legs were tied and a gag tied tightly over his mouth. Despite the pain he wiggled across the floor like a slithering snake until he bumped into a wall. Getting into a sitting position, he discovered it was a stone wall. The stone, cold and piercing, pressed into his back and with it the realization that cold stone in Egypt meant only one thing: a tomb. Had he been sealed away in a tomb? Would Holmes be able to find him? Solve the mystery of the missing doctor? Was he left to die where no man would find him for a thousand years?

He moaned, his head throbbing when he leaned back. But he was determined not to give up. So, what would Holmes do? Holmes would try to figure a way out, came the answer. *Yes*! But I am not Holmes! His brain cried out. Yet, if Holmes could believe there was a way out, then there must be. First he must remove the gag and after several painful minutes of struggling, the thing slipped from his chin and he was able to breathe freely once more.

Second, try to loosen the ropes around his wrists. He pulled and tugged but he was tied too tightly. Then he remembered the stones. Of course! Scraping the ropes against a sharp edge of a stone was a long, tedious and painful process, but Watson would not give up. He could feel the fibers fraying and breaking off in bits, the rope stretching and loosening around his wrists until finally, he was able to pull his hands free.

Free at last, he eased his arms around and rubbed the pin-prickling feeling away, then reached for the ropes binding his feet. He discovered his clothes were torn, elbows were bruised and bleeding and the lump on the back of his head had already crusted and dried. He sighed, leaned back exhausted. Everything seemed to swirl and darken as a wave of nausea took over and he slumped to the floor.

Chapter Twenty-Seven

"**I** tell you, he knows something and I mean to get at the truth!" shouted Holmes.

"Mr. Holmes, you must be mistaken!" Professor Princeton followed Holmes's retreating figure. "You can't do this I tell you. James is in a catatonic state. How could he have anything to do with Watson?"

"Get out of my way, Professor," Holmes said pushing Princeton to the side.

"Father! You must stop him!" cried Sharrey. "He cannot think James is in any way responsible. What has gotten into the man! Hurry, Minnie. He is so quick, we must run to keep up!"

Holmes threw aside the cloth blocking his way into James Princeton's tent. James lay on the cot, his arms at his side, his eyes closed. He had heard their approach and quickly jumped in before Holmes reached the entrance.

"Get up!" Holmes shouted. "Get up you charlatan!" He stormed across the space seizing James by the front of his clothes and jerked him from the cot. Behind him came the cries of the women shouting for help, shouting for Chibale! Shouting for someone to stop Holmes before it was too late.

"Father! Stop him, oh for goodness sake someone stop him!"

"James!" Minnie Rothman threw herself at Holmes, pounding with her fists but Holmes merely shoved her to the side. She stumbled backward against the cot.

"Stop! Please Mr. Holmes!" screamed Sharrey. "Please stop! James is innocent. He cannot have anything to do with Watson's disappearance."

"I disagree, Miss Princeton!" Holmes's fierce look stopped her and everyone else. He still gripped James by the front of his shirt and now shook him. "You will stop this charade, James! The game is up. We have known all along of your pretense to be in a catatonic state. We have known all along of your scheming with Miss Rothman to gain control of the ring and the box; of the mixture of poisons and the plotting to get your sister back to Egypt."

"Oh, James!" Minnie cried once more, her hands to her face. "We must tell them, James! We must! Dr. Watson has been kidnapped and may be seriously injured somewhere. We must find him, James. Please! It is all true, Mr. Holmes. Oh, James!"

Hanging limply in the grip of Sherlock Holmes, James suddenly found his ability to control his arms and legs and pulled himself away "All right!" he shouted. "It's true, all of it!" He reached for Minnie Rothman, pulled her into his arms and glared at the shocked faces surrounding him.

"I swear, please you must believe me, Father, I swear on my mother that I would never hurt Sharrey. You must believe me, Sharrey! You must believe me. I...I...I am so ashamed. It's just that I was getting so sick and tired of Egypt. I couldn't stand to look at one more dig site, to crawl down one more shaft of darkness, to be out here in the middle of nowhere where there was no civilization! Don't you see, Father! I needed the ring and the box to get some money to get out. I thought that if I could just have them even for a little while things would change for me."

"I do not understand," Peter Princeton muttered. "I thought you liked it here. I thought…"

"That's just it, Father. You thought. You always think for everyone else and you never let them have a say in anything. Sharrey always wanted to be here with you, to work alongside you. I know this because Minnie has told me. Yes, Minnie and I were in this together. It was during our visits to England that I met and fell in love with her, Father. Yes, Sharrey, I love Minerva Rothman. Have for a very long time. Yes, Sharrey, it was I who wrote to Minnie to convince you to come to Egypt because Father had told me about sending the ring and the box to you. I knew if you came here you would bring them back and I would be able to get hold of them.

"No, I know what you are thinking. I had nothing to do with any of the attacks on your life, Sharrey. I would never hurt you. You are my sister and I love you very much. I knew that if I asked you, you would give them to me simply because of that. I knew you did not know of their value, of the magical powers they hold. But I swear, I swear," James turned to Holmes, "that I had nothing to do with those attacks on anyone and I certainly know nothing of Watson's abduction. You have to believe me!"

"Oh, James, how could you?" Sharrey cried. "All of this just to get the ring and the box? All you had to do was ask me to come to Egypt and I would have flown on eagle's wings if I had them. All you had to do was ask for the ring and the box and I would have simply given them to you for I did not know what their true value was. But now that I know, now that I am aware of the wonders that can be accomplished with them, I must keep them. I must say how ashamed I am of you; of both you and Minnie. I have been attacked numerous times and if it had not been

231

for Berihun, I most likely would be dead. Poor Whittingham has now been attacked twice and he is a mere boy. And now Dr. Watson's life is in danger. All of this for a ring and a box that everyone has believed in a misguided notion of its wealth and power."

James crumpled to the cot ashamed. "I am so sorry for all of this. I have acted wrongly, I know that. I know that now. I have deceived you and Father but more than that, I have deceived myself and Minnie. Please," he looked from his father to Holmes. "Please let me help find Dr. Watson."

"I am afraid we must. We will need all the help we can get. Whittingham says they were attacked just as they were approaching the Red Pyramid. Colter has gone to assemble search teams of the workers. We will search in teams of four. We will need them when we find Watson in order to bring him back to safety, for I am sure he is injured," Princeton spoke.

"Oh Father, do not say such things," Sharrey cried.

"It must be expected. Watson was attacked and according to Whittingham put up a good fight. We don't know what happened later. But you," Holmes turned once more on James, "you we will deal with later!"

"Oh here you all are," Colter entered the tent. "I have all the workers assembled into teams…what's this? James!" he looked surprised.

"It is a long story, Colter and we have no time to explain. We must begin the search," Princeton said. "Send the men to search along the riverbanks and extend out into the desert area between the river and the dig site. We will search the Red Pyramid in that way we will be able to cover more ground. Tell the men if they find anything, anything at all, to send a runner to the pyramid."

They all left and the infirmary grew quiet. Whittingham and Berihum found themselves alone. The boy lay on the cot debating what to do. He'd made up his mind. He threw back the blanket and winced.

"Where do you think you are going, young one?" Berihun asked. "You have not yet had your wounds tended to."

"You heard them, Berihun. Watson is in danger and I have to help find him. The wounds can wait. They're not that bad anyway."

"I do not think they meant for you to be the one to go," Berihun said.

"But I have to go don't you see? It was me and Dr. Watson and Queenie. We were coming from Dashur together. He was with me, Berihun. He was with me when they took him. He fought them when they grabbed me but there was just too many of them. They knocked him on the head and he fell to the ground. I knew he was injured, Berihun. He got injured trying to help me. I have to help him back, don't you see? Besides, we were near that pyramid with the red coloring on it and I'll bet that's where they took him. That's what the 'red' meant."

Berihun eased up and asked, "Why do you believe they took him there?"

"Because, if I kidnapped someone, I would want to get rid of them as close as possible so I wouldn't have to carry the body all over the place. Well…not that I mean he's dead or anything, but that I just wouldn't want to keep it around, you know what I mean?"

"No, not really," Berihun rose from the cot and slipped on his sandals.

"Oh no, no you don't big man," Whittingham said putting his hands to Berihun's shoulders. "Dr. Watson would have my hide if he knew I let you out of bed with all those broken ribs."

"And you wish to stop me from searching for my friend even though you are as adamant about it as I? He is not only your friend, young one."

"I…I suppose you are right. Dr. Watson is a friend to all of us. Alright, but only if you promise to stay with me. That way if things get too rough, we can slow down, agreed?"

Berihun nodded. "As you wish. We will go together."

They slipped out of the infirmary tent, the cries and shouts of the searchers muted in the distance. Berihun clutched at his ribs and followed Whittingham to a narrow path behind the encampment. It was a short cut the workers used to get to the dig site that brought them to the west side of the Red Pyramid.

Chapter Twenty-Eight

Watson opened his eyes to a darkness that was absolute. He forced himself to stand, and leaning against the cold of the stone, he was brought up short in his memories of his childhood, of those long nights in the darkness alone and how he'd been afraid, even then. But then, he supposed, every child was afraid of the dark. Growing up into maturity usually surrenders those fears through reason and understanding. But here, in the endless black of the eternity he was facing, buried alive in the depths of only the Egyptian gods knew where, he concluded that it wasn't the dark that hurts you. It's what lurks in the dark.

The only way to find that out, was to move. He recalled an old school chum, a Gwen Donahue, an audacious and adventurous girl that dressed like a boy and dreamed about becoming a scientist-explorer. She would crawl through old caves and tunnels in pursuit of finding not yet discovered species of plant and animal life. She told him once when he refused to crawl in a particularly dark cave that the trick of survival in a cave was to follow the wall in one direction. Brush the wall with one shoulder or hand, and follow it around. Eventually you should come back to the point of beginning; or perhaps to another opening, a way out.

Alright Gwen Donahue, he sighed, here I go. With a deep breath, he put his left hand out in front of him and his right shoulder to the stone. If Gwen Donahue said it was so, then it was so. She always came out alive. He shuffled forward until he felt something beneath one shoe. It was the coiled up rope that had once bound his hands and feet. He took the rope and secured it around his shoulder with the thought it might come in handy. Several more feet he came upon a wall that turned to his left. Continuing, he came upon another wall and discovered he was making a circuit of what appeared to be a square chamber and that he would be coming to the third corner soon.

When his foot once again struck a wall, Watson knew he was right. He had been left for dead in one of the chambers of a pyramid. But which pyramid? There were several about. He knew that Holmes and the others were already searching, but with so much ground to cover and several pyramids to search, would they find him in time before the air in his chamber was depleted?

He didn't want to think about that so he continued until he stumbled against an obstacle in his path. Tracking its form, he found it went up at a steep angle and was several feet wide. Could it possibly be? A ramp! His heart beat furiously, and he retraced it back to the wall. Reaching up he discovering an opening an arm's length above his head. He scrambled up, crawling on his hands and knees where he crawled into a narrow passage, the walls so close, his shoulders brushed both sides.

A wave of dizziness swept over him, his head ached intolerably, the air was thin in the narrow passage and he could barely catch his breath. He tried to shake off the returning nausea, the image of Whittingham being struck down at the jetty was the last image before darkness enveloped him once more.

Chapter Twenty-Nine

"**Y**ou stay here, let me get around and check if anyone is there," the boy whispered. He crept along the base of the pyramid until he arrived at its eastern face. He saw a party of searchers in the distance, their torches flaring in the night. The scaffolding leading to the entrance was out in the open and seemed a long distance away, but there was no choice. They had to get there before those in the distance arrived. He ran back, finding Berihun leaning against the building, clutching his sides.

"Are you all right, Berihun?" he whispered.

"We forgot a torch. Once we get inside it is going to be very dark."

"We will manage. Hurry, let us go before we are discovered. A search party is coming. We must hurry!"

The voices of the search party could already be heard by the time they reached the entrance. It stood ajar and Berihun opened it with caution. Once inside, he pushed it closed once more. He put his hand on the boy's shoulder and whispered, "From here, we speak little. I will lead. Step slowly and cautiously and allow your eyes to adjust to the darkness."

Whittingham willingly allowed Berihun to take the lead. Somewhere in the distance, a single lamp had been left burning, the wick nearly gone, the flame just a pinpoint of light. His eyes fixated on that light for this was the first time he'd set foot inside of a pyramid, inside of a tomb that had housed mummies, real people had been buried here and the thought of the dead surrounding him, frightened him.

Whittingham held tight to Berihun's robes and wondered how the big man could see because his eyes never did seem to adjust to the darkness. Berihun came to a sudden halt.

"Mind your step, we have a great space here," the whisper in Whittingham's ear was barely audible. He took the boy by the hand. "We have entered a burial chamber. We will circle it together. Listen and feel, young one. We do not know if Dr. Watson is able to hear us." They circled the entire chamber coming back around to the narrow passage. Further along the passage once more Berihun stopped. "A second chamber. Listen and feel, young one."

Finding nothing in the second chamber, Berihun and Whittingham moved on. They came to a turn where it begun to rise on a sharp incline. It was steep and the walls began to close in upon each other and it was here that Berihun stumbled.

Whittingham lost his hold of the sleeve and a cry of alarm froze in his throat. "What! What happened?" He pressed against the wall, slowly sliding until he brushed against something. "Good lord, Berihun! I think we found him. I think we found Dr. Watson!"

Berihun reached in the darkness touching the boy's shaggy hair. And then he found another. "You are correct, young one. We have found him. And he is alive, thanks to all the gods. But wait! Someone is coming!"

"We should call for help," Whittingham said rising.

"No!" Berihun pulled him back down. "We know not if it is friend or foe. We shall bide our time. There is no point in rescuing Dr. Watson if we lead him back into the lair of the enemy, young one."

Chapter Thirty

"Colter and I will search inside the pyramid," Holmes was saying. "I think it's best if you all stay here."

"Are you crazy?" James shouted. "First you wish to blame me for what has happened then you refuse to allow me to make things right? I will be coming with you, Mr. Holmes. You cannot stop me."

"Nor me," Minnie was holding tight to James's hand.

"Well that settles that. We are all going into the pyramid," Sharrey said.

"Under the circumstances I do not feel that is a wise decision. There is still someone out there who wishes you harm, Miss Princeton," Holmes said.

"And I fear there always will be, Mr. Holmes. But that does not alter the fact that we will all be going into the pyramid with you, right Father?"

"She means business, Mr. Holmes."

Holmes glared from one to another. "Stay close, Miss Princeton, I prefer that you remain between myself and Mr. Mitanni. We must see to your safety even if you wish to disregard it. We have wasted too much time already."

Holmes put out an arm, stopping them near the entrance to the Red Pyramid. "Wait." He searched the ground intently then inspected the door. He said, "There has been recent activity here. There are footprints. Someone is inside."

Cautiously the entered and after lighting torches, followed to the large chamber, where earlier that day, Professor Princeton had brought them.

"Look here, Mr. Holmes, You can see there is nothing in this chamber but above us, in that corner just there, about twelve feet is another opening. We believe that to be the corridor leading to the actual burial chamber that was marked for the pharaoh, however it was never used. They could have put Dr. Watson there," Princeton pointed out.

"Hold my torch, Sharrey," Colter said. "Over here Holmes, I will give you a leg up."

Holmes stepped up and thrust the torch into the opening, cursing when the flame sputtered. "I need to get higher!" he called out.

"I don't think you need to get anywhere, Mr. Holmes."

Sharrey and Minnie screamed, nearly dropping the torches they held, no one had noticed the stranger that entered.

"Mother!" cried Minnie Rothman. "What are you doing here? What…what are you doing …."

"Quiet, Minerva. You have done quite well for me, my girl," Agnes Carmichael said.

"I don't understand, Mother. What…what are you doing with that gun?" Minnie stared in horror for she barely recognized the woman who was there. She stood at the entrance to the chamber wearing the shirt and trousers of a man, a large brimmed hat on her head. On her hip was a gun belt, slung low and fully loaded with bullets. The holster was empty, the glow of the torches glinted against the barrel of the gun she held

"You are such a foolish girl, Minerva. Come down, Mr. Holmes. All of you back up against the wall, there. That's right. I knew you had fallen in love with James and I was terribly disappointed. How could you? My own daughter in love with the son of the man who killed your father? But I soon saw that I could use that for my own benefit. Yes, you look at me as though I am crazy, but I am not. It has taken me many years of waiting in order to exact my revenge.

"You remember, don't you Peter? All those years ago when we were all friends and we all shared memories, worked at the same dig sites. Oh, I know, I know. Benedict really loved that wife of yours. She was so beautiful, so sweet, so kind and loving. I know he only married me because she had married you. Still, I loved him with all my heart and soul. And then you! You got him killed! I was left alone, Peter. Alone with a small child and I knew not where I was going to go with my life.

"But I did reap some satisfaction in knowing that Sari died soon after that daughter of yours was born. I tried then, Peter. I tried then to take away one of the things you loved most in this world but it seemed the gods of Egypt did that for me. I must admit that gave me some satisfaction, but not all. There still was the girl.

"And then you disappeared. No one knew where and how, but you were gone. Children, too. I lost tract of you and finally I myself had to return to England. Almost on a beggars fare but I managed. Oh, yes, I managed. I worked my way back up the social ladder until I managed to find a man no other woman wanted. Thaddeous Carmichael. Do you have any idea what an abomination of a man he is? Nothing like my Benedict, but he does have money. The root of all evil, Peter.

"And one day, Minerva came home from playing with the little girl next door and low and behold, Sharrey Princeton! Could it be? Why that gave me a renewed vigor in life to make it my quest to hurt you once more as you had hurt me. They became friends. You are such a lovely girl, Sharrey, so much like your mother. Beautiful, loving, caring. It made me sick!

"But I knew the secret. Oh, yes, I knew the secret. And much to my surprise, when Minerva came home and told me of the box and the ring I was ecstatic. Finally! Oh finally I would have my revenge. I would lure them all back to Egypt where you would finally lose the most precious thing in your life and I would finally gain my revenge.

"I want that ring and box. I want the power that Sari told me about. I want all that wealth and power of the barbaric tribes of Egypt and I want it now! Give me the box, Sharrey!" Agnes Carmichael shouted, waving the gun at the girl's face.

Sharrey drew back. "But I don't have it. You don't understand. You have a misconception of the ring and the box and the power they hold. It is not what you think!" she cried.

"I want that ring and box, Sharrey," Agnes said between gritted teeth.

"I cannot give you what I do not have!" she began.

"I want them, Sharrey, and to give you incentive," she fired the gun, a flame of red, a thunderous bang and Peter Princeton flew back against the wall and slid to the ground.

"Father!"

"I am all right, my dear. Shoulder…" he muttered.

"Mrs. Carmichael," Holmes made a move forward.

"I wouldn't do that if I were you, Holmes. There are still five bullets in this gun and there are only five of you left. I am an expert marksman."

"You can't imagine you will hit each of us surely," Colter said.

"I am a very good shot, I will tell you. So go ahead and try me."

"You really do not wish to do this," Holmes said.

"Oh yes I do. Do not give me this speech about the police and all the trouble I will be in. Pooh! Once I have possession of the ring and the box all the power will be mine. Do you think a small thing like your death would bother me?"

"You have held a grudge all these years? How could you, Mother!" Minnie cried clinging to James.

"Quiet girl, or James is the next shot. Peter Princeton ruined my life. He killed Benedict, the only man I truly loved. It tore my heart in two, taking away any reason for living, any reason for loving. I know I had you, Minerva, but it's not the same. My love for Benedict was so deep I would have gladly died with him. To see him lying in that hole with the shovel piercing his heart, I knew that day I had lost mine.

"The ring and the box, Sharrey, or James gets the next shot."

"I do not think that is going to happen, Mrs. Carmichael."

Again everyone jumped at the voice that had quietly stolen out of the shadows and up behind Agnes Carmichael. The hand that held a gun tapped her at the back of the head. "Give me the gun...please," said Chibale.

"Chibale!" James cried. "What are you doing! This wasn't in the plan!"

Chibale took the gun from Agnes Carmichael's grasp and tossed it behind him into the passageway. He shoved her headlong into the rest of the group that had now backed into the wall.

"The plan? You are all such fools!" Chibale snarled. He motioned his people in and two more surrounded the group with guns. "Did you think I would really truly help you to get your sister back for the ring and the box to be put into your hands? Are you that much of a fool? Ah, but then, I forget you are British and that makes you a bigger fool than this American woman."

"So it was you all along who made the attempts on Miss Princeton's life?" Holmes queried.

"Indeed, Mr. Sherlock Holmes," Chibale laughed. "I fear that I have bested you. The great Sherlock Holmes. Greatest detective in the whole of London yet here, in Egypt, he was never aware of the true enemy."

"Oh, I was aware, Chibale. It wasn't long for me to see that James and Minnie didn't plan all those attacks on Sharrey. Only an expert snake handler would have thought of the viper and the cobra as a means of murder and leave no clues. But after smelling the lingering aroma of a woman's perfume in my cabin back on the *Queen's Traveler*, I knew there were more interested parties to this ring and box than were originally thought."

"Did you think that I would allow such a treasure to escape? To be put in the hands of you British? You British have invaded our country once more and now wish us to follow your ways, your customs, your religions. My ancestors follow generations of the great Turkish commander, Muhammad Ali Pasha, whose people ruled this country effectively for many years. We are Egyptians, Mr. Holmes! Not French, not British, not slaves. We have a right to rule and manage our own country and our own affairs, and with the ring and the box in my possession, we shall take over and rule this country once more. Egypt does not belong in French or British hands."

"But if you are descended from Ali Pasha, you are not true Egyptian. You are Ottoman; a Turk. What gives you the right to rule these Egyptian people any more or less than the French or the British?" Colter argued.

"Quiet! It will be your head next, you who think you are better than others. You strut around, desecrating the sacred ruins of the ancient gods and the pharaohs, stealing the precious monuments and artifacts and showing them in your posh museums. What gives you the right? These are not your artifacts! These are not your gods! This is not your country!" shouted Chibale.

Holmes tilted his head and scratched his ear. He caught a movement in the dark behind Chibale and recognized the silhouette of Berihun. He shuffled his feet and cleared his throat hoping to create enough of a distraction for the big man to locate the gun that was lying in the passageway. When he saw the hand grasp the grip and pull it towards him, Holmes said, "Actually, it isn't yours either."

"Ah, but with the ring and the box in my possession, it will be," Chibale said.

"You cannot!" screamed Agnes Carmichael. "That ring and box are mine! I have worked hard for them! I have a right to them!"

"Mother, be quiet!" Minnie cried.

"Yes, be quiet, you foolish woman. But not so foolish as to set the great Sherlock Holmes on the wrong course, eh? I must thank you, Agnes Carmichael for your endeavors to retrieve the ring and the box have put him on the wrong trail, and I was able to carry my plans out without hindrance. But now, now I will not hesitate to shoot any one of you, or all of you. Now, Mr. Holmes, give me the ring and the box."

"I am afraid I cannot do that. I do not have them," Holmes shrugged.

"I am afraid you do. They are in your right pocket. And each time I have to ask you, I will have my men shoot one of these good people. Now! Shall we try this one more time. I want the ring and the box, Mr. Holmes."

Holmes stepped away from the wall, his gaze fixed on Chibale, but his attention fixed on the shadow in the passageway. The hand that reached out of the darkness holding the gun was not that of Berihun! He approached Chibale, reaching inside of his pocket for the ring and the box and saw the greed spewing from Chibale's eyes, his fingers stretched out greedily to grasp them.

In an instant, he threw himself at Chibale, knocking him to the ground. Two shots rang out swiftly one after the other and the two henchmen that Chibale had brought with him fell dead. "It pleases me that you are still such an excellent shot, Watson."

"It pleases me more that I am still alive to shoot, Holmes," Watson said entering the chamber leaning on the shoulder of Whittingham.

Chapter Thirty-One

Holmes stood at the rail of the *Queen Victoria* and watched the coastline disappear as the ship headed out to sea. Another long trip home but this time, it would be a quiet one. Just him and Watson. Yes, that man Watson. He turned and spied his friend further down the deck, sitting in a lounge chair beneath a sun umbrella. His eyes were closed and the blanket upon his chest rose with the steady rhythm of Watson's heart.

Watson. My God! He had come so close on this case to losing him! For many years Holmes had been alone. No friends. Family? Only his brother, Mycroft and Mycroft was as selfish with his time as Sherlock was with his. He'd managed quite well on his own solving cases, getting into danger, getting out of danger.

Then one day he was introduced to Dr. John Watson by a university colleague and they had moved into an apartment, sharing expenses. He hadn't noticed when it happened, when he considered Watson his colleague, his partner and dear friend.

Holmes went and sat next to Watson and looked upon him again. The wind blowing his hair revealing the healing wound on his head that would most likely leave a scar. The black and blue bruises slowly turning to yellow as the skin and blood vessels beneath began to heal. The brown eyes that stared at him from blackened rims

"What is it Holmes?" Watson asked upon finding Holmes staring at him.

"I was merely thinking about the case and how sorry I am, old friend, for not taking your concern about the sensations more seriously. It seems I have put your life in danger once more."

"Think nothing of it, Holmes. Danger is all a part of the work we do, is it not?"

"You are generous, Watson. It grieved me to realize that our friendship may have been lost over something as inconceivable as a curse."

"Why, Holmes, I believe that is the first time you have come dangerously close to calling me a friend," Watson laughed.

"It is the truth. You do mean a great deal to me, Watson."

Watson could see the difficulty Holmes was having for Holmes was never a man to reveal his emotions. "Well, everything worked out in the end, eh?" he said. "Miss Princeton and Mr. Mitanni will be married come spring. Everyone has forgiven James and Miss Rothman and they too will travel to England where they will be married and take up residence in their old homestead."

"I can't believe Professor Princeton refused to press charges against Agnes Carmichael. She would have spent the remainder of her life in a foreign prison for attempted murder. As it is, she will accompany James and her daughter back to England. Let us hope she can find forgiveness as the others have," Holmes said.

"I really did not like leaving Whittingham behind. I had taken a great liking for the lad. He showed such bravery at the landing, jumping into the fight with no regard for his own life. Poor lad."

"I don't think so poor, Watson. Professor Princeton has practically adopted the boy. He will make sure he receives a proper education and with the excitement and enthusiasm he shows, I am sure Whittingham will do the Professor proud as an archeologist, also."

"Chibale. What a character he turned out to be. Pretending to help James when all along he had his own hidden agenda."

"Yes. I rebuke myself sharply for not seeing the extent of his involvement sooner."

"Do not rebuke yourself, Holmes. We did what we set out to do. Protect Miss Princeton, her father and her brother. Now that the situation has been resolved, I am sure everyone will get back to everyday living."

"I'm afraid not so, for Miss Princeton. That woman has my utmost admiration. She was deserted as child, her life threatened over and over again, those she loved the most she found had betrayed her. Then discovering after all these years that she may hold the key to bringing about peace throughout the African nations. Yet, she has found it in her heart to forgive them all. She has a long hard road ahead of her, Watson, and those she must face will not be as forgiving."

"Yes, in striving for peace, it seems there is always war," Watson said. "The innocent will die again."

www.ingramcontent.com/pod-product-compliance
Lightning Source LLC
Chambersburg PA
CBHW030131180626
46812CB00002B/644